LT Mayle
Mayle, Peter
The Corsican caper

Seneca Falls Library
47 Cayuga Street
Seneca Falls, NY 13148

THE CORSICAN CAPER

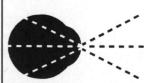

This Large Print Book carries the
Seal of Approval of N.A.V.H.

THE CORSICAN CAPER

PETER MAYLE

THORNDIKE PRESS

A part of Gale, Cengage Learning

GALE

CENGAGE Learning·

Farmington Hills, Mich • San Francisco • New York • Waterville, Maine
Meriden, Conn • Mason, Ohio • Chicago

GALE
CENGAGE Learning®

Copyright © 2014 by Escargot Productions Ltd.
Thorndike Press, a part of Gale, Cengage Learning.

LIBRARY OF CONGRESS CATALOGING-IN-PUBLICATION DATA

Mayle, Peter.
    The Corsican caper / Peter Mayle. — Large print edition.
    pages cm. — (Thorndike Press large print mystery)
    ISBN 978-1-4104-6780-5 (hardcover) — ISBN 1-4104-6780-5 (hardcover)
    1. Real property—Fiction. 2. Provence (France)—Fiction. 3. Large type books. I. Title.
    PR6063.A8875C67 2014b
    823'.914—dc23   2014015168

Published in 2014 by arrangement with Alfred A. Knopf, a division of Random House LLC, a Penguin Random House Company

LT

Printed in the United States of America
1 2 3 4 5 6 7 18 17 16 15 14

For Jennie,
once more with feeling

CHAPTER ONE

Francis Reboul sat in the sunshine, contemplating his breakfast: a shot glass of extra-virgin olive oil, which the French insist is so beneficial for *le transit intestinal,* followed by a large bowl of *café crème* and a croissant of such exquisite lightness that it threatened to float off the plate. He was sitting on his terrace, the shimmering sweep of the early morning Mediterranean stretching away to the horizon.

Life was good. Sam Levitt and

Elena Morales, Reboul's close friends and partners in past adventures, were arriving from California later in the day for an extended vacation. They had planned to sail around Corsica and perhaps down to Saint-Tropez then to spend some time at Reboul's horse farm in the Camargue and to revisit some of Marseille's excellent restaurants. It had been a year since they had seen one another — a busy year for them all — and there was a lot to catch up on.

Reboul put down his newspaper, squinting against the glare that bounced off the water. A couple of small sailboats were tacking their way toward the islands of Frioul. While he was watching them, Reboul's attention was caught by something that was beginning to appear from behind the headland. It gradually became more visible, and bigger. Much bigger. It was, as he would later tell Sam, the mother of all yachts — three hundred feet if it was an inch, sleek and dark blue, with four decks, radar, the obligatory helicopter squatting on its pad in the stern, and not one but two Riva speedboats in tow.

It was now in front of Reboul, no more than three or four hundred yards offshore. It slowed, and drifted to a stop. A row of tiny figures appeared on the top deck, all gazing, it seemed to Reboul, directly at him. Over the years, he had become quite used to this kind of scrutiny from the sea. His house, Le Palais du Pharo, originally built for Napoleon III, was the biggest private residence in Marseille, and the most glamorous. Everything from one-man sailboats to the crowded local ferries had stopped, at one time or another, for a long, if distant, inspection of Chez Reboul. Telescopes, binoculars, cameras — he was used to them by now. He shrugged, and hid behind his newspaper.

On board the yacht, Oleg Vronsky — Oli to his friends and numerous hangers-on, and "The Barracuda" to the international business press — turned to Natasha, the statuesque young woman whom he had appointed his personal first mate for the voyage. "This is more like it," he said. "Yes. This is more like it." He smiled, making the deep, livid scar on his cheek pucker. Apart from that, he would have been a good-looking man. Although a little on the short side, he was slim, his thick gray hair was cut *en brosse,* and his eyes were that shade of icy blue often found in people from the frozen north.

He had spent the past week cruising along the Riviera coast, stopping off to look at properties on Cap Ferrat, Cap d'Antibes, Cannes, and Saint-Tropez. And he had been disappointed. He was prepared to spend serious money, fifty million euros or more, but he had seen nothing that made him want to reach for his wallet. There were some fine houses, certainly, but too close to one another. The Riviera had become crowded, that was the problem, and Vronsky was looking for plenty of space and maximum privacy — and no Russian neighbors. There were so many of them on Cap Ferrat nowadays that the more enterprising locals were taking Russian lessons and learning to like vodka.

Vronsky took a cell phone from his pocket and pressed the single button that connected him to Katya, his personal assistant. She had been with him before the billions, when he was no more than a lowly millionaire, and she was one of the very few people who had his absolute trust.

"Tell Johnny to come and see me on the top deck, would you? And tell him to get ready for a quick trip. Oh, have we heard back from London yet?" Vronsky was negotiating to buy an English football team from an Arab consortium, not the easiest group of people to deal with, and he was becoming impatient. Somewhat encouraged by Katya's reply, he turned back to resume his inspection of Reboul's property, pushing his sunglasses up onto his head and adjusting the focus of his binoculars. No doubt about it, the setting was superb, and it seemed, from what he could see, that there were ample grounds around the house, undoubtedly enough for a discreet helicopter pad. Vronsky felt the first stirrings of what would quickly develop into a full-scale lust to acquire.

"Where to, boss?" Johnny from Jamaica gave Vronsky the benefit of his wide white smile, a gleaming gash across his ebony face. During his time as a mercenary in Libya, he had learned to fly helicopters, a useful addition to his other skills with weapons and the finer points of unarmed combat. A good man to have on your side.

"A short hop, Johnny. A little reconnaissance. You'll need a camera and someone who can use it." Vronsky took the Jamaican's arm and led him to a less crowded part of the deck.

Reboul dipped the final bite of his croissant into his coffee and looked up from his paper. The yacht was still there. He could see two figures in the stern busying themselves around the helicopter's landing gear before climbing in, and then the rotor blades began to turn. He wondered idly where they were off to, and returned to the news of the day as reported in *La Provence*. Why was it that, even with the season long since over, journalists devoted so much space to football players and their antics? He sighed, put aside the paper, and picked up the *Financial Times.*

The noise was sudden and shocking. Flying low, the helicopter was heading directly toward him. It slowed, then hovered above the terrace before making a couple of circuits around the house and its gardens. As it tilted to make a turn, Reboul could see the long lens of a camera poking out of the side window. This was unacceptable. Reboul took out his phone and tapped in the number of the chief of police in Marseille, a friend.

"Hervé, it's Francis. Sorry to bother you, but I'm being buzzed by some lunatic in a helicopter. He's flying low and he's taking photographs. Any chance of sending a Mirage jet over to discourage him?"

Hervé laughed. "How about an

official helicopter? I can send one of the boys out now."

But the intruding helicopter, with one final swoop over the terrace, was now on its way back to the yacht. "Don't bother," said Reboul. "He's gone."

"Did you see any of his registration markings?"

"No — I was too busy ducking. But he's going back to a yacht that's opposite the Pointe du Pharo, maybe heading for the Vieux Port. It's a huge, dark-blue thing the size of a *paquebot*."

"That won't be too hard to find. I'll look into it and get back to you."

"Thanks, Hervé. Lunch next time is on me."

■ ■ ■ ■

Vronsky leaned over Katya as she connected the camera to her computer and brought up the first of the photographs. Like many rich and powerful men, his grasp of the details of modern technology was sketchy. "There," said Katya, "just press this key to change the images."

Vronsky peered at the screen in silence, his shoulders hunched in concentration. As one image followed another — the perfectly proportioned architecture, the immaculate gardens, the absence of close neighbors — he started nodding. Finally he sat back and smiled at Katya.

"Find out who owns that house. I want it."

CHAPTER TWO

"Reboul would never sell. It is well known from Marseille to Menton that he loves his house. And he doesn't need the money. *Désolé.*" The speaker shrugged, and lit a cigarette with a gold lighter.

He was standing with Vronsky on the top deck of *The Caspian Queen,* which was paying a visit to the Cannes Film Festival. Vronsky's yacht was moored offshore, well placed to appreciate the distant glitter of the Croisette. He had chosen to introduce himself to Cannes by giving a party on board, organized by his public relations company, and not a single invitation had been declined. It was a fairly typical gathering of the usual characters found at film festival events: thin, overtanned women; stout men with the pallor that comes from spending too much time in darkened screening rooms; starlets and would-be starlets; journalists; and one or two festival dignitaries — to add a slightly formal touch of local color. And, of course, the gentleman in the white silk dinner jacket who was now having a discreet conversation with Vronsky.

He was, so Vronsky had been assured, the most successful and well-connected real estate agent on the coast. In his early days, his name had been Vincent Schwarz. This he had changed, for professional reasons, to the Vicomte de Pertuis — a title he invented that had nothing to do with noble birth — and during twenty years as a self-promoted aristocrat he had gained a near stranglehold on the top end of the coastal property market. Vronsky, he had to admit, was a challenge. So far he had proved to be a difficult and demanding client, turning up his nose at properties from Monaco to Saint-Tropez. But the Vicomte, encouraged by the thought of the agent's commission — a generous

5 percent — had persevered. Now, to his carefully concealed frustration, his client had found the house he wanted all by himself, without any professional help.

Circumstances like these demanded considerable finesse on the part of the Vicomte. He could scarcely expect 5 percent for merely supervising the transaction. Unforeseen difficulties and problems would have to be created — problems that could only be overcome by someone as experienced and wise in the ways of negotiation as the Vicomte. It was a principle that had worked for him several times in the past, and one which had prompted his negative response when Vronsky had asked him about

Le Pharo.

"How do you know he doesn't need the money?" Vronsky asked. His view was that there wasn't a man alive who couldn't be bought providing the price was right.

"Ah," said the Vicomte, lowering his voice to little more than a whisper. "In my profession, one needs above all accurate information, the more private and personal the better." He paused to nod, as if agreeing with himself. "I have spent years, many years, cultivating my sources. In fact, most of the properties I deal with never reach the open market. A word or two in the right ear, *et voilà.* A sale is made, always with the utmost discretion. My clients prefer it this way."

"And you feel sure that the owner would never sell?"

Again the shrug. "That would be my opinion, in the absence of more detailed information."

"And how do we get that?"

It was the question the Vicomte had been hoping for. "Of course, any inquiries would need to be carried out delicately, ideally by someone with a great deal of experience in these matters. Owners of important properties are never straightforward, often secretive, and sometimes dishonest. It takes someone with a shrewd eye and a keen nose to arrive at the truth."

It was the answer Vronsky had been expecting. "Someone like you, perhaps?"

25

The Vicomte fluttered a modest hand. "I would be honored."

And so it was agreed that the Vicomte would act as Vronsky's ferret, gathering information about Le Pharo and its owner. The two of them could then work out a plan of action. With this settled, they returned to the party on the main deck, Vronsky to play the part of the gregarious host, the Vicomte to continue his efforts to persuade a tipsy film producer from Hollywood to buy a charming little penthouse in Cannes.

A hundred miles along the coast, another, much smaller party was taking place to welcome Elena and Sam, who had just arrived after spending a couple of days in Paris.

Le Pharo was to be their base for the next three weeks, and Reboul had invited a few of the people whom Sam and Elena had met during a previous adventure in Marseille: the journalist Philippe Davin and his flame-haired girl-friend, Mimi; the redoubtable Daphne Perkins, this time without the nurse's uniform she had worn so effectively when called upon to foil a kidnapping; and the well-connected Figatelli brothers, Flo and Jo, who had come over from Corsica for the evening.

Once the ritual hugs and kisses of renewed acquaintance had been observed, reminiscence began to flow. Daphne, Champagne flute in hand, little finger elegantly cocked, listened to Jo as he described the latest developments in the Corsican underworld. And then, taking advantage of a lull in the conversation, she asked, "Whatever happened to that *ghastly* man?"

As everyone there knew, she was referring to Lord Wapping, the unscrupulous and crooked tycoon who had very nearly managed, by arranging for Elena to be kidnapped, to get the better of Reboul in a business deal. Daphne turned to Philippe. "I'm sure you've been keeping up with the case. Is he in prison yet? Is a life sentence too much to hope for?"

"He's not quite there yet," said Philippe. "He's using what we call the Serbian war-criminal defense

— a sudden and unexpected life-threatening illness that prevents him from being cross-examined. He's still holed up in a Marseille clinic, doing his best to look half-dead. The word is that he's bribing one of the doctors. But they'll get him in the end."

Elena shuddered, remembering the events, and Sam put his arm around her. "Take it easy, sweet-heart. That's one guy we won't be seeing again."

The mood was lightened by Mimi, with a rather sheepish Phi-lippe in tow. "Look," she said to Elena, "he's making an honest woman of me." She giggled, and held out her left hand to show the engagement ring on her third finger. It was the signal for congratulations and enthusiastic embraces. Reboul proposed a toast. Sam proposed a toast. Each of the Figatelli brothers proposed a toast. They floated into dinner on a tide of Champagne.

When they were all seated, Reboul tapped his wineglass for silence. "Welcome, my friends, welcome to Marseille. It is truly a pleasure to see you all, this time under more relaxed circumstances." He looked around the table, nodding at the smiling faces, before assuming a serious expression. "Now then, to business. Dinner tonight is a simple affair, but alternative arrangements can be made for anyone who is allergic to *foie gras,* rack of Sisteron lamb scented with rosemary, fresh goat cheeses, and *tarte Tatin. Bon appétit!*"

And with that, Reboul's housekeeper, Claudine, appeared with the maid, Nanou, from Martinique, to start serving.

The food was too good to be rushed, as were the wines, the conversation, and finally the fond farewells. By the time Elena and Sam climbed the stairs and reached their top-floor suite it was almost two o'clock.

While Elena was busying herself in the dressing room, Sam strolled over to the floor-to-ceiling window, with its view of the pools of light scattered across the water of the

Vieux Port. He wondered, not for the first time, what could induce otherwise sane adults to squeeze themselves into those tiny boats and endure discomfort and occasional danger on the heaving, unpredictable bosom of the sea. A sense of adventure? A desire to escape the cares of the world? Or was it just a refined form of masochism?

His musings were interrupted by the reappearance of Elena, her arms laden with the kind of expensive shopping bags that were sure to conceal even more expensive contents. "I wanted to show you what I bought in Paris while you were spoiling yourself with your shirt guy at Charvet," she said. And she carefully laid out on the bed a selection of underwear that would have been enough to stock a small boutique: silk, of course, some items in black, some in a very pale shade of lavender, all of them looking as though the slightest breeze would blow them off the bed. "There's this great little place on the Rue des Saints-Pères, Sabbia Rosa. Mimi calls it a girls' outfitters." She took a step backward and smiled at Sam, her head cocked. "What do you think?"

Sam ran his fingers over the fine silk of something so insubstantial he thought for a moment that it was a small handkerchief. He shook his head. "I don't know," he said. "I think I need to see them on, to make sure that they fit."

"Sure," said Elena, as she scooped them up from the bed and headed back to the dressing room. She looked over her shoulder, and winked. "Don't go away."

CHAPTER THREE

The letter had been hand-delivered earlier that morning, so Claudine said, by a very well dressed gentleman who had arrived in a Mercedes. He hadn't left his name.

Reboul opened the envelope, its inside lined with chocolate-brown tissue, and took out the single sheet of heavy, buff-colored paper. Instead of an address at the top, a discreetly embossed heading announced that the sender was the Vicomte de Pertuis. His message

35

was brief and to the point:

> I would be most grateful for a few minutes with you to discuss a matter of mutual interest and profit. I am entirely at your disposition as to a time and place to meet. Please telephone me at the number below to arrange a rendezvous.

This was followed by a one-word signature: *Pertuis.*

Over the years, Reboul, like most wealthy men, had received countless solicitations from people offering to increase his fortune by one shady means or another. Some had been amusing, others quite astonishing in their imaginative use of his money. This time, he found himself more than usually intrigued. Perhaps the title helped, although the aristocracy these days, God knows, had become thoroughly venal and commercialized. But one never knew. This might be worth a few minutes. He picked up his phone and called the number.

"Pertuis."

"Reboul."

The voice changed instantly, becoming unctuous. "Monsieur Reboul, how very kind of you to call. I'm delighted to hear from you."

"Obviously, I received your note. I'm free this afternoon around three, if that would suit you. I think you know where I live."

"Of course, of course. Three

o'clock it is. I look forward to it immensely."

Elena and Sam had spent the morning being tourists. Many changes had taken place in Marseille leading up to 2013, when it had taken its turn as the European Capital of Culture. And Elena, an avid collector of travel tips, had read about them all, from the transformation of the once shabby docks (*Le Grand Lifting*) to Pagnol's *"Château de ma mère"* becoming a Mediterranean film center. There were also new museums and exhibition sites, newly created gardens both wet and dry, even a glamorous glass *ombrière* to give visitors to the fish market some shelter from the elements, if not from the ripe language. All in all, there were enough novelties to occupy even the most fast-moving of sightseers for at least a month.

Sam did his best to keep up with Elena, but it was exhausting work. He looked with increasing longing at the cafés they rushed past until he could stay silent no longer. "Lunch," he said, his voice steely with determination. "We must have lunch."

He hailed a taxi, bundled Elena in, and told the driver to take them to the Vallon des Auffes, just off the Corniche. Elena put her travel notes in her bag and let out a long, theatrical sigh. "Culture is defeated, and gluttony wins again," she said, "and just when I was enjoying myself. Where are we going?"

"It's a little port with two terrific restaurants, Chez Fonfon and Chez Jeannot. Philippe told me about them: Jeannot for *moules farcies,* Fonfon for *bouillabaisse.*"

Elena looked down at her pale-blue T-shirt and cream linen skirt. "I'm not dressed for *bouillabaisse.* How about the *moules*?"

The Vallon des Auffes is a pocket port, too small to accommodate any but the most modest boats. Without doubt, the best place to appreciate the miniature but highly picturesque view is the terrace at Chez Jeannot, and Elena settled into her seat with a little sigh of satisfaction. "This is cute," she said. "Maybe you were right after all."

"Sorry about that. I won't let it happen again." Before Elena had a chance to roll her eyes — her standard response to Sam's attempts at sarcasm — he had buried himself in the wine list. "Let's see: a vivacious little *rosé*? Or perhaps a crisp and beautifully balanced white, with just a hint of impertinence, from the vineyards of Cassis?"

Over the years, Elena had become used to Sam having *bon viveur* moments as soon as he set foot in France. It was part of the travel experience. "Do you think they have French fries to go with the mussels?"

"*Pommes frites,* sweetheart, *pommes frites.*"

"Sam, you're behaving like a dictionary. Don't be a pain."

"A pain? I'm thirsty, I'm hungry, and my feet hurt, but otherwise I'm the soul of charm and good humor. Now, what's it to be? Pink or white?"

When the *rosé* arrived, Sam raised his glass to Elena. "To our vacation. How does it feel to be back here again?"

Elena took a sip of wine and held it in her mouth for a moment before swallowing. "Good. No — better than good. It's lovely. I've missed Provence. I know how much you like it, too." She took off her sunglasses and leaned forward, her expression suddenly thoughtful. "How about getting a little place here? You know, just for the summer. Somewhere to keep your espadrilles."

Sam raised his eyebrows. "You wouldn't miss summer in L.A., when the smog is at its most beautiful?"

"I guess I'd survive. Sam, I'm serious."

"OK, that's settled." He smiled at Elena's startled reaction, and raised his glass again. "That was easy. As a matter of fact, I was going to suggest the same thing. I could learn to play *boules*. And you could learn to cook."

Before Elena could think of a suitably crushing reply, the *moules farcies* arrived, the mussels cooked with herbs, garlic, and, according to the waiter, *beaucoup d'amour;* the *frites* fried twice to make them crisp on the outside, soft on the inside. To accompany the food there was an excited but inconclusive discussion about property in Provence: the merits and drawbacks of the coast versus the country, a village house in the Luberon or an apartment in Marseille. Over coffee, it was agreed that they would contact a couple of real estate agents to help them look around. When the bill came, Elena insisted on paying. She planned to frame the check as a souvenir of the day they had made their decision.

When they returned to Le Pharo

at the beginning of the evening, it was to find Reboul still fuming. He had received a visit, he told them, from someone he described as a used-car salesman masquerading as a Vicomte, who had said that he had found an extremely rich buyer for Le Pharo: a man, he had said, with the deepest of deep pockets. It's not for sale, said Reboul. Not for fifty million euros? Don't you understand, said Reboul, it's not for sale. Aha, said the Vicomte, but it is well known that there is a price for everything. It is possible that I could persuade my client to dig even deeper into his pockets.

"And that's when I showed him out," said Reboul. "There's a price for everything, is there? *Quel culot!*

What a nerve!"

"Well," said Sam, "I guess that's one real estate agent we can knock off the list."

Reboul paused, corkscrew in hand. "What do you mean?"

"We decided at lunch. We'd like to try and buy a little place over here."

Reboul's face lit up. "Really? How wonderful. Now that really does deserve a drink." He put the corkscrew to work on a bottle of Chassagne-Montrachet. "This is the best news I've had in weeks. Where do you want to be? What can I do to help?"

The Vicomte, to his credit, was a very resilient man. Besides, he had come up against similar protestations many times before, most of which had vanished when their speaker was faced with a big enough check. And so, when he was reporting back to Vronsky on *The Caspian Queen,* he managed to present an appearance of guarded optimism.

"Of course he said he wasn't interested in selling. That's what they all say at first — it's an old trick to get the price up. I must have heard it dozens of times." The Vicomte smiled, nodding his thanks for the glass of Champagne that had been put in front of him by Vronsky's chief steward. "I've found that it's usually best to leave them to think about it for a week or two before getting back to them. You're not planning to sail off somewhere, I hope?"

Vronsky shook his head. "I don't like unfinished business. That property is perfect for me, and I won't be leaving Marseille until it's mine."

CHAPTER FOUR

Reboul had persuaded Elena to persuade Sam to put aside his horror of all things that float and come on a cruise around Corsica. His boat, as he had been at pains to explain to Sam, was built for comfort rather than speed; as another inducement he promised that they would never be out of sight of land. In fact, it was generally accepted, according to Reboul, that the very best way to see Corsica was to sail around it. Many of the prettiest little beaches were inaccessible by car and, at this time of the year, deserted. And, as Elena said, it does a girl good to have a beach all to herself. She was in her element — barefoot, clear-eyed, her skin the color of dark honey, her disposition angelic, her pleasure contagious. How could Sam resist? Confirmed landlubber though he was, he had to admit that sailing had its moments.

They had moored overnight in the port of Calvi, with a view of the massive Citadelle that had kept watch over the town for six hundred years. Dinner had been taken in a restaurant two steps from the quay: a fine *daurade royale,* the fish celebrated by its admirers as "the playboy of the Mediterranean." It had been cooked in a salt crust and served with a pungent aioli. To follow there was *brocciu,* the creamy local cheese best enjoyed with a generous helping of fig jam. Now they were back on the boat, drowsy and replete, their skin still tingling from the day's sun.

Reboul had left Elena and Sam on deck, leaning back in their chairs counting the stars. When he reappeared, it was with a bottle and three glasses. "We must finish as the Corsicans do," he said, "with a little nightcap that will make us sleep like babies." He placed the bottle on the table. In its appearance, it was as far as a bottle can get from the gilded extravagances that are so often used in the presentation of after-dinner drinks. It was devoid of printed label or ornate stopper. There was a label of sorts, stuck on sideways, with a single handwritten word: *Myrte.* And there was a stopper — a cork, darkened with age, that looked as though it had seen service in several other bottles. The overall effect would never have won any prizes for elegance.

Reboul set the glasses in a row and started to pour. "This is made by the farmer who lives near my aunt in Speloncato. Myrtle berries, macerated in a mixture of *eau-de-vie* and sugar, with a touch of lemon and a couple of cloves." He slid two glasses across the table.

Elena sipped once, then again. "Ah, yes," she said in her best wine-taster's voice. "I think I detect a hint of cloves." She smiled at Reboul. "I could get to like this a lot. It's lovely — sweet, but kind of peppery. Do you think your aunt's farmer would make some for me?"

The next morning, they sailed south. Reboul wanted them to see the village of Girolata, accessible only by sea or mule track, where Sébastien, an old friend, had decided to spend the summers of his retirement. To keep himself amused, he had opened a bar on the beach, hired a pretty local girl as bartender, and assumed the modest responsibilities of chef. Since there was only one dish on the menu — the local *langouste* — his kitchen duties gave him plenty of time for his favorite hobby, which was sitting in the sun.

He was standing at the water's edge to welcome them as they came ashore — wiry, tanned to a crisp, his face a network of wrinkles relieved by a wide white smile. He embraced Reboul, kissed Elena's hand, shook Sam's, and led them up the beach toward a low, open-fronted shack with tables and chairs arranged under faded canvas umbrellas. A sign hanging above the bar read Le Cac Quarante and, in smaller letters, *Les chèques sont pas acceptés.*

"Cac Quarante — that's a pretty weird name for a bar," said Elena.

"Is it some kind of Corsican specialty?"

Reboul grinned. "Not quite. It's the French equivalent of the Dow Jones index — the movement of the most important forty stocks on the Bourse. That's where Sébastien used to work."

They were settling themselves around the table and studying the handwritten, postcard-sized wine list when Reboul's phone rang. He left the table and strolled down the beach while he took the call. When he came back, it was with a scowl on his face. He was shaking his head as he sat down. "You won't believe this," he said. "That was Claudine. That real estate agent has just turned up with Vronsky, that

Russian maniac with the helicopter. They told Claudine that I'd said they could look around the house. While she was talking to me, they'd slipped away and gone into the living room. So I told her to call the police and have them kicked out." He shook his head again. "Unbelievable."

Sam took a bottle from the ice bucket and poured a glass. "This might help. It's Canarelli, Sébastien's favorite *rosé.*" Sure enough, the first long, considered swig seemed to have a calming effect on Reboul. "Tell me, Sam," he said, "what would happen if someone did that in America?"

"Well now," said Sam, "you have to remember that in the States, a house is not a home without a gun. So I guess we'd shoot him. That usually works."

Reboul smiled, his good humor restored. "I must remember that."

The *langoustes* were fresh, firm, and sweet, served with a mayonnaise almost thick enough to need a knife, made with egg yolks and extra-virgin Corsican olive oil. A second bottle of wine was ordered, and the conversation turned to Elena and Sam's plan to buy a small place in Provence — nothing grand, but as Elena said, with *beaucoup de charme.*

"I think I should warn you," said Reboul, "that those three words are memorized at birth by all Provençal real estate agents. Charm is the great excuse for dark rooms, tiny windows, low ceilings, suspect plumbing, rats in the cellar, bats in the bedroom, and anything else that might be seen as a disadvantage. If the property is really on its last legs and falling to pieces, it has *un charme fou* — a crazy charm. And, as if that's not enough, it will also have 'enormous potential.' So don't be surprised if the agent offers to lend you rose-colored spectacles." He paused for another sip of wine. "Anyway, when we get back I'll find a couple of names of people for you to contact."

Three sunny, lazy days later, they were back. It had been, for all of them, a brief but magical vacation from real life, and it left them with a feeling of benevolence toward the rest of the world. This, of course, couldn't last.

Real life was lying in wait.

Elena, who had left her electronic links to the office at Le Pharo, opened her BlackBerry to find a dozen messages from clients she had blissfully forgotten. Sam, a man who was far too busy enjoying life to contemplate death, found an extremely stern e-mail from his lawyer, who professed himself to be deeply concerned about Sam's repeated failures to make out a will. And Reboul, despite himself, had become increasingly taken up by thoughts of Vronsky; not only thoughts, but questions. When a

man takes such an aggressive interest in your home, it's only natural
to want to know more about him.

Fortunately for Reboul, there was
Hervé, Marseille's chief of police,
whom he had contacted recently
about Vronsky's helicopter. As Reboul had found several times in the
past, Hervé's tentacles seemed to
reach everywhere — the underworld, the government, Interpol,
even deep within the local chamber
of commerce. The two men met for
lunch three or four times a year to
exchange gossip and favors, an arrangement that suited them both.

"Well, *mon vieux*," said Hervé,
"what have you done now? Too
many parking tickets? Assaulted a
politician? Been caught pinching

girls' bottoms again?" As his laughter came down the phone, Reboul could picture Hervé's face — round, smiling, and cheerful, a misleading face that concealed the tough and determined officer Reboul knew him to be.

"I need a little information," said Reboul. "Remember the business with the helicopter? Well, I think the guy who organized that has been snooping around again. While I was away, he got into the house for a guided tour. I'd like to know a little more about him. His name is Vronsky. He's Russian, and he's rich. Very rich."

"Let me see what I can find out. Rich Russians in Europe aren't too difficult to track. I'll try to have something for you in a couple of days. Meanwhile, don't do anything I wouldn't do, *d'accord*?"

CHAPTER FIVE

The early evening calm at Le Pharo
— the hour of *l'apéritif* — was
disturbed by the sound of a motor-
cycle's engine. The rider, a burly
policeman in highly polished boots,
parked his machine carefully, re-
moved his helmet and placed it on
the saddle, rang the front door bell,
and stood to attention. He had
been told that this was a very important delivery, ordered by the
chief himself, and that all the nice-
ties should be observed.

Claudine opened the door. The policeman saluted. "For Monsieur Reboul," he said, handing over a manila envelope.

"Merci, monsieur."

"De rien, madame. Bonne soirée." Mission accomplished, he saluted again before roaring off down the drive.

Claudine immediately took the envelope to Reboul, who slit it open and took out three sheets of paper. The first was a handwritten note from Hervé:

Cher ami,

I am taking the small precaution of using the old-fashioned way of communicating, with pieces of paper. As you know, nothing electronic is completely private these days, and I would prefer that this doesn't end up on the Internet.

As you will see, Monsieur Vronsky has had an interesting career. What strikes me is the high mortality rate of his business partners. Although nothing has been proven, I don't believe in coincidence, and I regard these deaths as a serious warning. I strongly recommend that you have nothing to do with this man. He seems extremely dangerous.

Amitiés,
H

Reboul poured himself a fortifying shot of Scotch and turned to the other two pages, which were typewritten.

VRONSKY, Oleg. Born St. Petersburg January 4, 1970. No record of any formal education.

From 1989 until 1992, he served in the army, first as a private, later as a sergeant commanding a tank squadron. On returning to civilian life, he and an ex-army friend, Vladimir Pugachev, used their military connections to set up as arms dealers, first in the Balkans and later, as their business flourished, in West Africa. Business continued to grow, but Pugachev met his death in unexplained circumstances while on a sales trip to Ouagadougou, with his share of the company passing to Vronsky. Rumors of foul play were vigorously denied.

Vronsky continued to prosper. After selling his African business to the up-and-coming dictator Marlon Batumbe, he returned to Russia and founded PRN (Prirodni Resursi Neogranichenyi — in Russian it stands for Natural Resources Unlimited), a company formed to exploit mineral deposits found in the southern Urals. Several profitable years followed, and Vronsky was able to engineer a deal with a bigger company owned by Sergei Popov. The merger was less than two years old when Popov met his death in unexplained circumstances while attending a bauxite seminar in Magnitogorsk, with his share of the company passing to Vronsky. Rumors of foul play were vigorously denied.

Increasingly rich, well-connected, and powerful, Vronsky spread and diversified his empire, with exploitation businesses in the Arctic and the Amazon basin. There was also an apartment building on New York's Park Avenue, bought in conjunction with Jack Levy, a Manhattan real estate developer. It was widely agreed that Levy's suicide — he jumped off a thirty-eighth-floor terrace — was a considerable loss to the community. However, it was a substantial gain for Vronsky, who took over Levy's share of the building.

Vronsky seems to have no permanent address, preferring to use his yacht, *The Caspian Queen,* as his headquarters. He stays in hotels when he travels. Details of his personal life are somewhat limited, but one or two have emerged. Although he has been seen with a variety of beautiful women, his only marriage ended in divorce, and he has no children. His hobbies include bear hunting, chess, and ballroom dancing.

"You're looking very thoughtful, Francis." Sam had stopped in the doorway of the living room. "Nothing wrong, I hope?"

"No, no. I've just been finding out about that Russian. Get yourself a drink and read this." He passed the documents to Sam, who poured a glass of wine and made himself comfortable on the sofa.

"That's quite a C.V.," Sam said a few minutes later. "Not a guy to go into business with, is he? When he lays someone off he means it." Sam shook his head. "Losing three partners? I wonder how come he's never been nailed. Or at least reprimanded for carelessness."

"Don't forget he lost them at three different times in three different countries. Can you imagine the police in Africa, Russia, and

America getting together?" Reboul gathered up the papers and put them away in a drawer. "Enough of him. Where is the lovely Elena?"

"Trying to improve upon perfection." Sam shrugged. "I've noticed that when she's here in France, she takes twice as long as usual to make up and get ready. Three times as long when she's in Paris, where she says the level of competition is that much higher."

Reboul smiled. "The ladies. How dull life would be without them. Do you know where you're going tonight?"

"One of Philippe and Mimi's friends, Yves, is a great cook. He and his wife, Ginette, have just been awarded a Michelin star, so we're going to their restaurant to celebrate. How about you?"

Reboul grimaced and shook his head. "A romantic evening with my accountant, going through figures. Next month we have to file returns for the wealth tax — something you Americans have very wisely chosen to avoid. It seems to get more complicated every year." His face brightened as he looked toward the door. "Ah, here she is — La Bomba. Ravishing, my dear, ravishing."

Elena performed an abbreviated curtsey. "Thank you, kind sir." She was indeed looking ravishing, in a vanilla silk dress that showed off her dark hair and glowing Corsican tan. Sam had to admit that the wait had been worth it.

In the taxi going to the restaurant he told Elena what he'd just learned about Vronsky. She could hardly believe it. "Do you think he seriously expects Francis to sell Le Pharo?"

"I'm not sure," said Sam. "But a guy with that much power and money isn't used to taking no for an answer. He thinks he can get away with anything, because that's the way it's been for years. And he has a pretty scary track record. I think we're going to have to keep a close eye on him."

CHAPTER SIX

It was gala night at Le Palais du Pharo. Six months previously, Reboul had allowed his good nature to get the better of him and had agreed to act as host for a dinner in aid of a local charity, Les Amis de Marseille. The charity had been sponsored by a committee of local businessmen, whose aim was not entirely without self-interest; charity, after all, begins at home. But the cause was worthy and locally very appealing: to promote

Marseille as a coastal destination with events to rival Cannes with its film festival, Nice with its flower festival, and Monaco with its tennis and its Grand Prix.

What could Marseille offer that those other destinations didn't? Yacht racing, music and theater festivals, a floating casino, world championship *boules,* and a competitive water-skiing tournament were all under consideration as possible attractions. But ambitious schemes of this kind take money to set up, and the evening at Le Palais du Pharo, with dinner at a thousand euros a head, was to get the ball rolling and to pass the collection plate.

Reboul had done Les Amis proud.

The vast back terrace of Le Pharo had been turned into something between a small forest and a giant bower. There were olive trees, lemon trees, and clumps of black-stemmed bamboo, all in huge terracotta pots, and all decorated with garlands of tiny lights. Placed among the trees were twenty six-seater tables, each with its thick linen cloth and napkins of true Marseille blue, its candlelit lanterns, and its centerpiece of white roses. A small band, installed on a dais in one corner, was playing old French favorites — "La Mer," "La Vie en rose," the theme from *Un Homme et une femme.* Even nature had made a contribution: the air was soft and still, the sky an expanse of black velvet pricked by stars. It was, as one of the early guests said, *un décor magique.*

The host and his team were having a glass of Champagne to help them prepare for the evening's events. Elena was in what she called ceremonial black, although she declined to say exactly what kind of ceremony she had in mind. Sam had plenty of ideas, but was told to keep them to himself. The newly engaged Mimi and Philippe held hands while they drank their Champagne, and Reboul and Sam were resplendent in their white dinner jackets.

"Well," asked Sam, "have you worked out your speech?"

Reboul winced. "I agree with the

man who said that the rules for making a good speech were simple: stand up, speak up, and shut up. So I shall keep it short and sweet." His eye was caught by a figure coming through the crowd. "Ah, there she is — my social mentor."

Marie-Ange Picard was a specialist organizer of events of this kind. A slim, blonde woman in her thirties, she too was squeezed into a little black dress, this one cut to display a generous *décolleté* with her official plastic name card strategically placed where it would receive maximum attention. Introductions were made by Reboul, and for a moment or two Elena and Marie-Ange looked each other over like two boxers preparing to go into the ring. "What a darling little dress," said Marie-Ange. Elena inclined her head and smiled. Not as little as yours, she thought. Maybe next time you should go for something that fits.

Marie-Ange turned her attention to Reboul, inching closer to him with every question. "*Alors,* Monsieur Francis. Have you got everything you need? The notes for your speech? Are you happy with the seating arrangements at your table? Would you like to go over the guest list again — there have been one or two late additions." By this time, Marie-Ange's bosom was almost pressed against Reboul's chest.

He took a step backward, escaping the fog of perfume, and looked around the crowded terrace. "Have all the tables been taken?"

"The last two or three went yesterday," said Marie-Ange. "One of them went to a Russian gentleman. He bought all six seats."

Reboul frowned. How many Russian gentlemen prepared to spend six thousand euros on dinner were there in Marseille? "Who is this man?"

Marie-Ange consulted her guest list. "A Monsieur Vronsky," she said. "Perhaps you know him?"

Reboul shook his head. "I haven't had the pleasure."

Marie-Ange led Reboul over to the dais. The band ended Piaf's old classic, "Non, je ne regrette rien," with a flourish, and Marie-Ange took over the microphone.

"Ladies, gentlemen, friends of Marseille — a warm welcome to you all. I can promise you an evening you will never forget." She glanced down at her notes. "After dinner — and what a dinner" — she paused to kiss her fingertips — "there will be an auction, an auction *de luxe,* to tempt you into extravagance. But extravagance in a most worthy cause. First, we have a weekend for two at Le Petit Nice, with its three Michelin stars, its magnificent sea views, and its legendary *bouillabaisse.*" Another pause for fingertip kissing. "Six bottles, selected from our host's personal cellar, of Lafite Rothschild 1982, one of the great vintages of this magical wine. Next, for all you football fans — four tickets to the Club des Loges for all of next season's Olympique de Marseille home matches. Finally, a rare opportunity to acquire a truly extraordinary car: the vintage Bentley R-Type, bought by King Farouk to celebrate his becoming an official resident of Monaco in 1959."

Marie-Ange turned to Reboul. "And now," she said, with the air of a conjurer about to produce a particularly handsome white rabbit from her hat, "I would like to ask our most generous host for the evening, Francis Reboul, to say a few words — a very few, he has asked me to tell you — to welcome you." After leading the applause, she passed the microphone to the next, somewhat reluctant, speaker.

In his brief but charming remarks, Reboul thanked his audience for their support and emphasized that this evening was just a start — the first step on a journey that he hoped would end with a spectacular addition to the delights of his beloved Marseille. "But I'm sure you're all hungry," he said, looking toward the summer kitchen, "and I can see my friend Alphonse the chef tapping his watch. In my experience, he is not a man to be kept waiting. *Allons, mes amis! À la bouffe!*"

There were well over a hundred people settling themselves at their tables, and Reboul knew most of them personally: a wide selection of local businessmen and their wives; Hervé, the chief of police; luminaries from the chamber of commerce; Gaston, the fixer; Madame Spinelli of the Women's League of Marseille and Bruno, her considerably younger partner; the executive committee of the Olympique de Marseille football club; and a sprinkling of socialites, comparing tans and jewelry. In other words, there was everyone who counted in the social hierarchy of Marseille.

And some who didn't — not yet, anyway. At a prominent table, already making short work of a magnum of Dom Pérignon, was a group that Marie-Ange described, in a whispered aside to Reboul, as "the Russian contingent." There was Vronsky, in a plum-colored velvet smoking jacket, with Natasha on one side and Katya on the other; the Vicomte de Pertuis and Madame la Vicomtesse, a fashionably anorexic woman brandishing her cigarette holder with dangerous abandon; and, lolling back in his chair with the light glinting on his sunglasses, a rather glamorous young man with implausibly ash-blond hair, dressed from head to toe in black leather.

Reboul was making his way back to his table after greeting some friends when he heard his name called. He turned, and found himself looking into the chilly blue eyes of Oleg Vronsky.

"Ah, Monsieur Reboul. I am Vronsky."

For once, Reboul's habitual good manners deserted him. "I know," he said, and turned away.

Vronsky caught up with him and took hold of his arm. "We should talk," he said. "It could be very interesting for you."

"I doubt it," Reboul said, brushing away Vronsky's hand and returning to his table, leaving the Russian standing alone, the object of some curiosity to those at nearby tables. He recovered, pushing a waiter aside to get back to his seat.

He was scowling as he sat down. "Arrogant French shit," he said to the Vicomte. "Who does he think he is?"

At Reboul's table, a very similar comment was made, although the nationality of the arrogant shit had changed.

"I can't believe it," said Sam. "I hope he apologized for invading your house?"

Reboul shook his head. "It wasn't a long conversation." He turned to Elena, who was sitting next to him. "I'm sorry, my dear. Forgive me. Let's not spoil the evening."

CHAPTER SEVEN

As Reboul explained to Elena, the dinner menu he had worked out with his chef, Alphonse, was a completely Provençal affair. "We start," he said, "with melons from Cavaillon, a town that supplies the finest melons in France. They are so good that Alexandre Dumas had a 'books for melons' deal with Cavaillon back in the nineteenth century. In fact, the town archives still have a selection of books that Dumas sent in exchange for his dozen melons a year." He stopped to take a sip of Champagne, and realized that the others at the table had stopped talking to listen. "And the juiciest, tastiest melons, the ones we're having tonight, are the *melons de dix,* with ten ribs that cut into ten perfect slices."

Elena looked across the table. "Sam, I hope you're taking notes. You're in charge of the kitchen when we get a place here. OK, Francis, what's next?"

"*Daube Avignonnaise,* a summer stew, lamb marinated in white wine, and so a little lighter than the red-wine beef *daubes* of winter. It's served with pasta and a white Châteauneuf-du-Pape. Then cheeses, from our good friends the local goats, and to finish, a favorite of mine — strawberries from Carpentras, with a sauce invented by Alphonse, or so he says. It's a mixture of cream and yogurt, with a touch of balsamic vinegar. *Voilà* — that should put everyone in a good mood for the auction."

Over the melons, which were indeed perfumed and juicy, Philippe, who had just spent two days reporting from Cannes, answered the usual questions about the film festival. Which stars did he meet? Did he actually see any films? Is this year's favorite leading man the tall heartthrob he appears to be on-screen, or is he, as one unkind columnist put it, "a dwarf with acne"?

Finally, when Reboul asked Philippe if he had taken away an overall impression of his two days, the latter nodded. "Judging by what I saw, face-to-face conversation is finished," he said. "All I saw, everywhere, were groups of people who were together but not talking to each other, not even looking at each other. They were all staring at their cell phones. The only real conversations I had were with the barman at the Martinez."

This gloomy assessment was interrupted by the summer *daube,* which was generally agreed to be a triumph: light, tender, and tasty. "Elena, are you taking notes?" Sam was wiping the last traces of sauce from his plate with a piece of bread as he asked the question.

"I just told you — you're going to be in charge of the kitchen."

"I only do melons," said Sam. "After that, I delegate."

Elena rolled her eyes, as Sam knew she would, and the conversation turned to house-hunting, and the absolute necessity of a large wine cellar and a soundproof guest room. With the arrival of the strawberries, the irritating behavior of Oleg Vronsky came up. Sam was of the opinion that he was a real estate stalker, and should be officially warned by the police to stop making a pest of himself. Reboul was more philosophical. "Although," he said, "if he bothers me again I shall have to do something about it."

But what? Before they had a chance to explore the possibilities, Marie-Ange had once more taken to the dais, her appearance marked by a drumroll and a discreet adjustment of her bosom. It was time for the auction.

First, there was the weekend for two on offer at Le Petit Nice, known throughout France, as Marie-Ange reminded her audience, for its superb position overlooking the sea, for its stylish and comfortable rooms, and most of all for its three-star cuisine. Quite carried away by enthusiasm, she went into raptures about the joys of eating on the terrace, the legendary *bouillabaisse,* the sublime olive oil (a special supply for the hotel) —

and then, with yet another kiss of her wilting fingertips, she opened the bidding.

It started at a very modest 500 euros before quickly going up to 2,000, then 2,500. "You must try harder," said Marie-Ange. "This is not merely a fabulous, *fabulous* weekend — it's an investment in the future of your city." After a late flurry of bids, the weekend was finally sold for 5,000 euros. The buyer was a prominent local businessman well-known for his roving eye, and Reboul had to suppress the desire to ask him if he planned to take his wife or his mistress with him on the weekend.

Onward went the auction and upward went the bids — the six

bottles of Château Lafite going for 20,000 euros, while the VVIP tickets for the O.M. matches, after more persuasion from the dais, went for 50,000. Marie-Ange was pleased, but she was not finished. Taking a restorative sip of Champagne, she moved on to the main item of the auction, the vintage Bentley. This had been parked for the occasion in front of the house, where it had attracted considerable attention from the guests as they arrived. It was a magnificent machine — pearl gray, with leopard-skin upholstery, and a speaking trumpet with a solid gold mouthpiece for passing instructions from the rear seat to the chauffeur. As Marie-Ange said, in a not-too-subtle reminder of the identity of the previous owner, a car fit for a king.

"For this unique car," she said, "we are hoping that you will make a special, special effort. Let me say again, it is for the good of Marseille. So, ladies and gentlemen, please exercise your checkbooks. Who will start the bidding?"

Conversation had stopped, and the terrace was quiet enough to hear the scrape of a chair being pushed back over the flagstones. Vronsky stood up, one arm raised, the fist clenched. "For the good of Marseille," he said, pumping his fist, "I bid one million euros."

After a stunned few seconds, the terrace exploded with applause, led by Marie-Ange, who skipped across to the beaming Vronsky and planted a kiss on each of his cheeks.

Philippe, his journalistic instincts aroused and quivering, had taken out his notepad and had started to scribble. "This would make a nice little story for *La Provence,*" he said. He turned to Reboul. "You don't mind, do you?" Reboul shrugged and smiled. "Of course not. Why don't you do an interview with him? And if you get the chance, point him in the direction of Moscow."

The headline on page three of *La Provence* read "Le Meilleur ami de Marseille" — Marseille's best friend — and featured a slightly

fuzzy photograph, taken with Philippe's cell phone, of Vronsky, his
arms folded across his chest, leaning up against his newly acquired
Bentley.

After a few kind words about the
charity and a description of the
evening's auction, the article moved
on to a short question-and-answer
session. What did Monsieur Vronsky plan to do with the Bentley?
How did he happen to be in
Marseille? Did he plan to spend
more time here? When the answer
to this was an emphatic yes, the
next question almost asked itself:
Where was he going to live? "I have
my eye on a property," Vronsky
said, "and that's all I'm going to
say at the moment."

■ ■ ■ ■

Reboul snorted as he put down the newspaper. "Cheeky bastard," he said to Sam. "He has his eye on a property, has he? Did you see him snooping around after the dinner? He was almost measuring the curtains. *Quel culot!*" He stumped off, his body rigid with indignation.

Sam saw Elena coming across the terrace after her morning dip in the pool, and poured her a cup of coffee. "What's the matter with Francis?" she asked. "He barely managed to say good morning. Have you said something to upset him?"

Sam held up his hands in surrender. "Not me — it's that Russian." He passed over the paper and pointed to Philippe's piece. "Read the last couple of sentences — it's no wonder Francis is in a lousy mood."

Elena read them and pushed the paper away. "The nerve of the guy. Does he think he can bully Francis into selling him the house?"

Sam shrugged. "Take a look at his career. He's done business in some tough places competing with some tough people, and he's either beaten them or gotten rid of them. One way or another, he comes out on top. He apparently has unlimited money and a great deal of power, and he's used to getting what he wants. Now he wants Le Pharo, and he seems to be the kind of guy who'll do anything to get it.

Look at his record. For now, I think he's sure that all he has to do is throw enough money at Francis and he'll get the house. I guess that's how it works in Russia."

"That's how it works in the States too, Sam. Or hadn't you noticed?"

Sam shook his head and grinned. "Too busy looking at you, my sweet. Now, what would you like to do today? Sightseeing? House-hunting? Shopping? Nude sunbathing?"

"I'd like to do something that would cheer Francis up."

"Great idea," said Sam. "Nude sunbathing it is."

Elena sighed, and observed a moment of silence. When conversation was resumed, they decided to take

Reboul out for a long, relaxed lunch, an idea that lifted his spirits immediately. Sam called Philippe and asked him to join them at a restaurant called Peron, a reservation was made, and, just after noon, they got into the car and set off.

They were rounding the first bend when they had to come to an abrupt standstill, the way blocked by Vronsky's Bentley parked in the middle of the driveway. Vronsky was standing outside the car with the glamorous young man who had been at his table for the dinner, the one wearing head-to-toe black leather. Today he wore a sleeveless white T-shirt that set off his deeply tanned and muscular arms, suede hot pants, and biker boots, with a long-lens camera slung around his neck.

Reboul got out of the car and Vronsky, all smiles, came over to meet him. "My dear Monsieur Reboul," he said, "I do hope you can forgive us." He waved a hand toward his companion. "Nikki, my bodyguard, wanted to take a few photographs of Le Pharo to send to his mother. She lives in Minsk, and has never seen architecture like this in her life."

Before Reboul had a chance to speak, Vronsky moved closer and his voice became confidential. "I must confess that I've fallen in love with your glorious house, and I will pay you anything you ask for it." He looked at Reboul and nodded, his frosty blue eyes narrowed to slits. "Anything."

Reboul summoned up as much self-control as he could. "I've told your agent, and now I'm telling you, my house is not for sale. I think you'd better leave. Now."

Vronsky took a deep breath. Nobody had spoken to him like that since his time in the army. "Very well," he said as he turned to leave. "But I hope you won't regret that decision."

Reboul was fuming as they followed the Bentley down the drive, and Sam did his best to lighten the atmosphere with his observations about Nikki the bodyguard. "How about that guy," he said. "He dyes his hair and shaves his legs." He grinned and turned to Elena. "Maybe I could pick up a few style tips. How would I look in hot pants?"

"Sam, believe me. You don't want to know. But the leg shaving could work."

By the time they reached the restaurant, Reboul seemed more like his old self. "I'm glad we're seeing Philippe," he said. "I'd be interested in what he thinks about Vronsky after doing that interview." He shook his head. "I need a drink."

The four of them were sipping their *rosé* and admiring the menu when two passing waiters stopped in their tracks. *"Putain!"* said one of them to the other. "Look at that."

And there, creeping out from behind the headland, was the massive bulk of *The Caspian Queen.*

Reboul almost choked on his wine. "It's that goddam Russian again — I'm sure he's following us."

Sam patted his friend on the shoulder. "Relax, Francis. We're safe here. He could never find a parking spot."

Philippe, who had been unusually silent, cleared his throat as he looked around the table. "I have a confession to make." He paused, clearly a little uncomfortable. "He's invited me onto his boat."

Three pairs of eyebrows went up as Philippe continued. "He called me and said how much he liked the piece about the auction. He wants me to do a profile of him — 'to introduce myself to my new neighbors, the people of Marseille,' he said." Philippe stopped to take a drink. "That was when he suggested I should stay on the boat for a day or two, to get to know him. He didn't want to make a date, though — said he was too busy. But he'd call when he was ready."

"What did you say?" asked Reboul.

"My first reaction was to tell him to get lost. Then I thought — well, if he's trying to screw you, it might be worth having someone in the enemy camp. Maybe he'd let something slip that would be useful."

Reboul nodded slowly. "That's

not a bad idea." He turned to the others. "What do you think?"

Elena and Sam agreed. There was nothing to lose.

"Tell me, Philippe," said Reboul, "you've spent more time with Vronsky than we have. What did you think of him?"

"He reminded me of politicians I've met. You know, arrogant. Very pleased with himself. Not a man to cross, I'd say. But he does seem to love what he's seen of Marseille. Particularly your house."

CHAPTER EIGHT

The subject of the conversation at
Peron was sitting on the VIP deck
of his yacht having a serious discussion with his bodyguard. During
the years they had been together,
Vronsky had come to rely on
Nikki's assistance in solving stubborn problems. The Russian had
found that Nikki's solutions, practi-
cal if sometimes brutal, were always
effective. This latest situation, like
others in the past, would undoubtedly be resolved. But how?

Vronsky was beginning to accept that it would take more than money, however substantial, to induce Reboul to change his mind and sell his house. He was clearly rich enough not to be influenced by cash.

"How about sex?" Nikki suggested. This was a weapon he had used often to good effect. "There are dozens of good-looking hookers in Cannes for the festival. An assignation in a hotel room — photographs, blackmail. That could be arranged."

Vronsky shook his head. "Forget it. This is a rich man who has lived in Marseille for years. If he feels like a change from his mistress, he wouldn't have any trouble finding someone to oblige."

"Boys?"

"I don't think he's the type." Vronsky grinned. "You should know."

Nikki pouted.

Vronsky went over to the rail and took in the view — the flat sheen of the Mediterranean, the old port of Marseille, and, high on its own clifftop, Le Palais du Pharo. Vronsky had to admit that the house had turned into an obsession. He thought about it — and how it would be to live in it — constantly. He felt he deserved it, after all he had achieved. And, to add to his frustration, it was unique, both in its style and in its setting. He would never find another property like it.

But if money, sex, and blackmail wouldn't persuade Reboul, what would?

Nikki came over to join him. They were both aware that there was another, more certain option, one that they had used in the past. "I was thinking," said Nikki, "about that guy in New York, the one who fell off his terrace and made such a mess on Park Avenue."

"Tragic accident. Very sad." There was a brief pause while the two men struggled to control their grief. "But why do you ask? Do you have something in mind?"

"Perhaps another tragic accident. After all, accidents happen all over the world." Nikki turned away from the view to look at Vronsky, his expression innocent, his eyebrows raised and questioning.

"Let me think about it," said Vronsky.

"Of course, we would need to know much more about Reboul's habits — where he goes for amusement, if he has a bodyguard, if he has any dangerous hobbies, who he sleeps with, where he eats, that sort of stuff. You never know what might be useful."

Vronsky sighed. This would all be so much easier in Russia.

Later that evening, as the lights went on in Marseille, Vronsky was back on deck, smoking a cigar and gazing once again at Le Pharo. If anything, it looked even more seductive at night, with the façade bathed in a soft wash of light. Vronsky could imagine himself there — the genial host entertaining elegant women and their wealthy and influential escorts at dinner. And then perhaps a little dancing — there was plenty of space at Le Pharo for a ballroom. All that was standing between him and this delightful existence was that stubborn idiot of a Frenchman.

Nikki's solution, death by accident, was, as Vronsky admitted, a last resort. But he had run out of other resorts, and now the decision was simple: either let Nikki loose or say good-bye to any chance of realizing his dream. As for the larger question — was it worth kill-

ing for something you wanted? —
Vronsky had answered that many
years ago, when sound business
reasons had required the removal
of troublesome colleagues. Any
moral qualms had long since disappeared.

Vronsky yawned, stretched, and
made up his mind. He slept particularly well that night.

Reboul settled into the passenger
seat while Olivier, his chauffeur,
put the finishing touches to the
adjustment of his sunglasses before
joining the early morning traffic
heading toward the Vieux Port.
They were going to the small,
shabby building where Reboul had
his office. Shabby though it might

be on the outside, visitors were always astonished by the interior, which was sleek, comfortable, and modern. The only vintage item among the Eames chairs and polished teak desk and tables was Reboul's secretary, a sixty-year-old treasure named Madame Giordano, who had been with him since he was a young man starting off in business thirty years ago. Madame G, as she was usually known, adored Reboul, ran his professional life with brisk efficiency, and generally treated him with the patient indulgence of a mother toward a much-loved errant child.

Olivier slowed down and was about to pull up outside the office when Reboul tapped him on the shoulder. "Keep going," he said. "There's something I want to check out. See that white Peugeot behind us? It was parked on the road outside Le Pharo when we left. I noticed it because his side mirror is almost falling off, and it's been repaired with black tape. It's still with us, and that's quite a coincidence. I have a feeling we're being followed."

Olivier glanced up at the rearview mirror. "You want me to lose him?"

"No — just make life a little difficult for him."

There was nothing Olivier liked better than a chase, and he set off on a tour of the side streets, doubling back on his tracks and jumping the occasional light. The Peugeot was never more than fifty yards behind them.

"This guy knows how to drive," said Olivier. "And you're right. He's following us, no doubt about it."

They eventually lost him by turning off the Boulevard Charles Livon at the Cercle des Nageurs, a private swimming club not far from Le Pharo, where nonmembers driving grubby white Peugeots were not admitted. Reboul called Madame G to say that he wasn't coming in, then settled at a poolside table with a cup of coffee. He was thoughtful, trying to think who might be following him, and why. Taking out his phone, he started to call Hervé, then cut the connection, chiding himself for being a nervous old woman. Even so, he told himself, it was not surprising he felt uncomfortable.

Later, in the Vieux Port, Nikki was seated at a café table enjoying the afternoon sun — a more conventional Nikki, having replaced the hot pants and biker boots with the uniform of a gentleman on vacation: clean and well-pressed cotton trousers, a white linen shirt, and a wide-brim Panama hat. He was with a Marseillais named Rocca, a shadowy figure who made his living snooping for lawyers, or doing "legal research," as he preferred to call it. He had been hired to follow Nikki's invented client, a man of considerable wealth whose wife suspected him of maintaining a mistress and a love nest. Divorce and a multimillion-euro settlement were possible, but first it was necessary to find some evidence.

"Well," said Nikki, "where did he go?"

Rocca shrugged and took a long pull at his *pastis.* "Where didn't he go? All around the backstreets, down to the docks, and then up near Le Pharo, which is where I lost him; no, where he lost me. He went into this place, the Cercle des Nageurs — very chic, members only. They wouldn't even let me into the parking area. So I waited outside until I came down to meet you. No sign of him."

"Bastard," said Nikki. "Obviously meeting his mistress. What am I going to tell his poor wife?" Another shrug from Rocca. "Do you think he knew he was being followed?"

"Don't think so. But if you want me to keep tailing him I'll need another car, something that isn't a white Peugeot falling to bits."

Nikki nodded, and pushed an envelope across the table. "Rent another car. Make a list of where he goes, and call me at the end of every day."

Elena and Sam had decided to spend some time house-hunting, and had made an appointment to meet a real estate agent based in the Luberon, about an hour's drive from Marseille. It was an area, so Philippe had told them, well known for its spectacular landscapes and its charming medieval villages. And equally well known, in these days of celebrity worship, for welcoming the invasion each summer of *les people* — movie stars and directors, rock musicians, members of the Paris elite, the occasional high-ranking politician — all hoping to be recognized despite their impenetrable sunglasses. Philippe had told them that the celebrity magazine *Gala* maintained a special summer correspondent to lurk in the neighborhood, watch the rich and famous at play, and, with a bit of luck, catch them behaving badly. But, he added, if one avoids this group and their goings-on, the Luberon is a calm and beautiful spot.

"Well, it certainly is beautiful," said Elena. They had driven through the Combe, a narrow, twisting road that cuts through the hills to link the more fashionable northern side of the Luberon with the quieter, less famous villages of the south. They were meeting the agent at her office in Gordes, sometimes called the capital of the summer *beau monde,* an absurdly picturesque arrangement of limestone buildings softened by centuries of sun and the mistral wind. The village sits on top of a hill, surrounded by long and lovely views, and it had recently come to life with a vengeance after the winter hibernation.

English, American, German, and Japanese tourists, students from the nearby art school at Lacoste — they were all there, cameras clattering as they discovered yet another quaint cobbled passageway or an obliging inhabitant to pose with. Elena and Sam threaded their way through the crowd to find the agent's office, tucked away in one of the steep streets that lead off the Place du Château.

The office was approached through an archway that gave access to a tall, narrow house festooned with wisteria, its shutters half-closed against the sun. The polished brass plaque on the front door announced that this was the headquarters of Verrine, Immobilier de Luxe, and in a glass-fronted display case on the wall next to the door were photographs of a dozen handsome properties, none of them with any indication of price. This, as Elena and Sam were to discover, was a delicate matter best left for discreet conversation.

While they were looking at the photographs, the front door swung open, and there, in all her considerable glory, was Madame Verrine herself, the agent, who complimented Elena and Sam on their punctuality, which, as she said, was not normal in Provence. Later, Elena would describe Madame Verrine as a ship in full sail — tall, buxom, in her fifties, her considerable size draped in billows of brightly colored silk, her neck and wrists twinkling with gold jewelry, her plump face a testament to the rejuvenating properties of good cosmetic surgery.

"OK," she said as she led the way into her office. "You are American, yes? So we speak English." She waved them into two armchairs before arranging herself at her desk.

"That would be great for me," said Elena.

"No problem. Here in Gordes, English is the second language. So, first I must ask if you have a budget."

"It's very flexible," said Sam. "Depends on what we see. As you know, buying a house is an emotional business. If we fall in love with something — well, the sky's the limit. Let's not worry about money."

Money was exactly what Madame Verrine wanted to worry about, but she bore the disappointment with a brave face, opened a thick album and placed it in front of them. "These are some of my properties," she said, tapping the first few photographs with a crimson talon. "Stop me when you see something that interests you." But that was easier said than done. She took off, her descriptive juices flowing, on a sales pitch that defied interruption. As Reboul had predicted, there was *charme fou* in abundance, closely followed by houses with extraordinary potential, houses offering wonderful investment opportunities, houses owned by celebrities trading up or divorced couples trading down. They were all, without exception, *affaires à saisir,* to be snapped up before July and August, when the hot money came down from Paris and people would be fighting — literally *fighting* — over such highly desirable properties.

At the end of the morning, reeling from Madame Verrine's nonstop barrage, they made their escape, promising to think things over and get back to her.

"Wow," said Elena, "my first French real estate agent. Do you think they're all like that?"

"It's a very competitive business. I've seen five agencies right here in the village. So I guess you need to be pushy by nature. If you're not, you should go into something easier, like crime. Now, shall we try that place Philippe suggested for lunch?"

La Vieille Grange, after fifty years of service as a storage barn and tractor garage, had been taken over by a young couple, Karine and Marc, and transformed into a restaurant of the old-fashioned kind: a short, modestly priced menu of fresh, local produce, local wines and cheeses, and a total absence of pretension. Any waiter wearing white gloves would have felt deeply uncomfortable. In fact, the waiter's job was already taken by Karine's uncle Joseph.

The building, long and low, was at the end of a narrow dirt track that led off the road linking the villages of Lourmarin and Lauris, on the more peaceful south side of the Luberon. A frequent passer-by might have noticed that every lunchtime the field next to the barn was crowded with cars, which spoke well of Marc's cooking.

Sam parked the car next to an elderly Renault and noticed, as they made their way toward the barn, the absence of large shiny cars or foreign license plates. It seemed that this was very much a place for locals. And it was a boisterous babble of thick local accents that greeted them as they pushed open the door. Although it was barely past noon, the restaurant was already almost full. A smiling Karine found them a corner table for two, gave them each a small menu, and recommended a carafe of *rosé,* as it was such a hot day.

The long rectangular room was pleasant and uncluttered, devoid of the fussy touches of the interior decorator, with ambience and décor being provided by the customers. The tables and chairs were plain and functional, the tablecloths were paper, the wineglasses were sturdy tumblers. "My kind of place," said Sam. "I'm sure a lot of these people are regulars — they all seem to know each other."

Elena poured their wine from a glazed jug, beaded with moisture. "I haven't heard anyone speaking English," she said. "Do you get the feeling we're the only foreigners here?"

Sam was nodding as he looked up from the menu. "This is *definitely* my kind of place. See? They have *velouté d'asperges* — and this is the best time of year for asparagus. And then there's roasted duck breast stuffed with green olives. That's it for me." He put down the menu, picked up his glass, and raised it to Elena. "Who needs a kitchen when there are places like this?"

Elena smiled. Sam's enthusiasm, when he was having one of his *bon viveur* moments, was infectious. "You sold me," she said. "I'll have the same."

With those vital decisions made, their conversation turned to Madame Verrine and her seemingly inexhaustible supply of properties. It only took a few minutes before Elena, somewhat hesitantly, leaned across the table to take Sam's hand. "I hope this isn't going to be a big disappointment," she said, "but looking at all those houses on their own in the countryside suddenly made me realize something: I'm a city girl — I need people and streets and activity, the sounds of a city, the buzz. I don't know if I could deal with all that peace and quiet. I know it's beautiful, and I think it would be great for weekends, but . . ." She paused, squeezing Sam's hand. "Well, you know what I mean."

Before Sam could reply, Uncle Joseph came with a basket of warm bread, the first course, and a murmured *bon appétit* as he placed two deep soup bowls in front of them. In fact, soup would have been too modest a word to describe the contents, subtly perfumed and visibly smooth, like pale-green velvet, decorated with a generous swirl of cream.

"First things first," said Sam, who didn't look too surprised by Elena's confession. "Eat this while it's warm, and then we'll get back to real estate." He bent his head over the bowl, inhaled, raised his eyes to heaven, stirred in the cream, and took his first spoonful. "Sublime. Not only sublime, but as this is your first taste of asparagus this year, you're allowed to make a wish. Old Provençal tradition."

Elena was too busy to reply, and it wasn't until their bowls were empty and the last drops wiped up with bread that she spoke. "You don't *seem* too disappointed, Sam. Are you?"

"No. No, I'm not. The way I look at it, Provence is the treat of a lifetime, but it has to be *our* treat. I'm fine in a city, as long as we can get out to places like this once in a while. So, how would you feel about an apartment in Marseille?"

Elena's expression was all the answer Sam needed, and for the rest of the meal — the admirable duck breast, the smooth, slightly moist goat cheese, the feather-light apple tart — Marseille was all they talked about. Or rather, Elena talked and Sam listened. The city, so she said, was perfectly placed: only an hour away from wonderful countryside, right next door to Cassis, which they both loved, not too far from Saint-Tropez and the Riviera if they felt like a dose of glamour and, as a huge bonus, Francis and Philippe were there to show them the ropes.

With that settled, they drove back to Marseille in the highest of high spirits that often accompany the making of an extravagant decision while under the influence of an excellent lunch and a glass or two of *rosé*.

CHAPTER NINE

"Guess what, Francis — we're going to be neighbors." Reboul looked up from his desk as an excited Elena burst into the room and bent over to kiss him on the forehead. "We've decided to look for a place in Marseille. Isn't that great?"

Reboul rose to his feet, a broad smile lighting up his face, and returned the kiss. "That makes me very happy," he said. "And, by an amazing coincidence, there is a bottle of Champagne out on the terrace waiting to be drunk. Where's Sam?"

By the time Sam joined them on the terrace the bottle had been opened and the glasses filled. "A toast," said Sam, raising his glass. "To Marseille, to good times, and most of all, to our friendship. Thank you, Francis."

"It's my pleasure," said Reboul. "I'm delighted, but tell me — whatever happened to life in the Luberon?"

"Ah. Well, there's no doubt it's the most beautiful spot, really lovely. But we've realized that we're not cut out for the country. We're city people. Elena's absolutely right — a quiet life in a remote farmhouse watching the lavender grow would probably drive us crazy."

Reboul nodded. "I know what you mean. My old farm in the Camargue is bliss for three days. After that, I start inviting the horses in for a drink."

As they continued to talk about their plans — and Elena had at least a hundred questions to ask about everything from the absolute necessity of a sea view to the merits of various neighborhoods — it became apparent that Reboul had something on his mind. He had become preoccupied, and more and more subdued, so much so that Elena stopped in midsentence.

"Francis, are you OK?"

Reboul shook his head and sighed. "Forgive me. It's that idiot

Russian — I've just had a report back from the people in Paris who have been doing a background check on him and his business methods, and it's not good news." He got up and went inside, returning with a slim folder. "All the details are in here, but what seems to happen is that most of his deals have had fatal consequences for someone."

He opened the folder and spread the pages out on the table. "It's not just those so-called accidents in Africa and Russia — I remember we made a joke of it at first — but it's also happened in the Amazon and the Arctic. Competitors in both places suffered severe side-effects." He looked up and drew the side of his hand across his throat. "And then there was the incident in New York." He paused to take a sip of Champagne.

Sam was frowning. "Where were the police when all this was going on?"

Reboul tapped the page in front of him. "Investigations were carried out, or so it says here. But there was a problem, and it was always the same problem: in every case, Vronsky was never in the same country at the time these fatalities occurred, sometimes not even on the same continent." Reboul shrugged. "So how do you prove a crime has been committed by someone who wasn't there? You can have as many suspicions and theories as you like, but that's not enough. You need proof."

Elena took the Champagne from its ice bucket and topped up their glasses. "These guys who did the report — what do they recommend you do?"

"Stay away from him. And don't forget that he seems to be at his most dangerous when he's somewhere a long way away." Reboul closed the folder and did his best to smile. "So I'd better keep an eye on his travel arrangements."

It was only later, over dinner, that Reboul mentioned the car that had followed him in the morning. He tried to make light of it, but there were three worried people who went up to bed that night.

Optimism returned with the morning sun, to Sam at least. He was careful not to seem too cheerful in front of Reboul, but he wasted no time putting forward his idea. "Let's change places for the morning," he said. "Lend me Olivier and your car, and we'll see if our friend in the Peugeot wants to play hide-and-seek today. If he does, I'd like to have a word with him."

Reboul leaned across and patted Sam's cheek. "You're a dear friend, Sam. Thank you, but no. It's my problem, and I don't want you getting involved."

"Francis, you don't understand — a little challenge like this is something I enjoy. Besides which"

— he wagged a finger at Reboul — "it gets me off the hook with Elena. She and Mimi have planned a fun-filled day with Marseille's real estate agents, and after Madame Verrine I don't think I can take any more enthusiasm. A pleasant, peaceful drive would do me a world of good." He paused, and thought he could see that Reboul's resistance was beginning to weaken. "So, do we have a deal?"

"But won't this fellow know it's not me in the car?"

"Not a chance. All he's seen is the back of your head from thirty or forty yards away. It's the car he'll recognize." Sam grinned. "Admit it — you've run out of arguments."

Reboul stood up and stared out

the window. "Very well. But Sam, you must promise me you won't do anything dangerous."

"Yes, Daddy."

Olivier was delighted at the prospect of a break from his normal shuttle service to and from Reboul's office.

"If this guy does follow us," said Sam, "I want to find a place where we can stop and have a chat with him. Can you think of somewhere that would work?"

Olivier adjusted his sunglasses while he thought. "*Pas de souci,* not a problem. I have an idea," he said, taking out his phone. "Just give me a minute."

When he'd finished he explained

his idea. The call had been to
Ahmed, Le Pharo's large and in-
timidating gardener. If they were
followed, he would call Ahmed
again, give him detailed instructions as to where they could meet,
and tell him to follow the follower,
who would then become the filling
in a three-car sandwich. "After
that," said Olivier, "it's just a question of picking a suitable spot, *et
voilà.*"

Sam was impressed. "Have you
done this sort of thing before?"

"Oh, once or twice. Before working for Monsieur Francis, I was a
cop. In fact," he said, putting a
finger to his lips, "I've still got my
gun. But that's strictly *entre nous.*"

As they pulled out of the drive-

way, Sam peered around the newspaper he was using to hide his face
to see if there was any sign of a
white Peugeot. "I don't see him,"
he said.

"Don't worry. If he's a pro, he'll
have changed cars. And he
wouldn't have waited in the same
place."

By now, Olivier had turned off
into the labyrinth of small streets
behind the Vieux Port, his eyes
flicking up every few seconds to the
rearview mirror. With a sudden
nudge of the accelerator, he crossed
an intersection as the lights were
changing before slowing down.
"Ah, there you are, you bastard.
Don't look around," he said to
Sam. "It's a gray Renault with

rental plates, about twenty meters behind us." Olivier took out his phone, called Ahmed, and told him to be outside the Banque de France on the Rue Paradis in ten minutes, and to follow the gray Renault that would be a few meters behind them.

"Now," said Olivier, "I don't want to lose him, and we've got a few minutes to kill. We'll take the long way around to the Rue Paradis, and that should do it."

They arrived to find that Ahmed, who had double-parked in front of the Banque de France, was looking under the hood of his pickup for some imagined mechanical fault. Olivier flashed his lights. Ahmed closed the hood, got back into the pickup, and pulled into the traffic two cars behind the Renault.

The three-car procession, widely spaced and traveling at an unhurried pace, made its way through the center of town. "Remember when you stayed at Monsieur Francis's other house the last time you were here?"

"Is that where we're going?"

"Not quite. At the end of that road there's a *rond-point* — a traffic circle. It looks like it goes somewhere, but it doesn't. That's the end of the road."

They drove on, into the 7th and 8th *arrondissements,* where many of Marseille's wealthiest residents live in their large houses behind high stone walls. There was less traffic now, and the Renault had dropped back, frequently out of sight on the narrow, twisting road. They passed Reboul's old house. "Not long now," said Olivier. He called Ahmed and told him to close up on the Renault.

Another two hundred meters, and one last bend. The road had narrowed to a single lane before ending in the small traffic circle. The Renault came around that last bend and stopped short, behind Olivier. Ahmed's pickup came to a halt immediately behind the Renault. There was nowhere for the driver to go. He was trapped.

Sam and Olivier walked back to the Renault, where Ahmed was waiting, his arms crossed, glaring at Rocca, the driver. He seemed to have shrunk behind the wheel, his face the picture of apprehension. Olivier opened the driver's door and, in his most threatening police manner, told Rocca to get out. "Nobody ever comes down here," he said, "so we can have a nice quiet chat without being disturbed. *Bon,* now let me see your driver's license, and give me your cell phone." For a split second Rocca might have considered protesting. But with three large and unfriendly men looming over him, he thought better of it, and did as he was told. Olivier noted the license details and handed it back. The phone he kept.

Olivier, prompted by Sam's questions, proceeded to give Rocca a grilling. Who had hired him? How did Rocca contact him? Where did they meet? When was their next rendezvous? Why were they interested in Reboul? What exactly were they looking for?

To many of the questions Rocca had no answers, and it became clear that, apart from the cover story, he had been kept in the dark. After twenty frustrating minutes they were ready to let him go.

With the engine running and his window open, Rocca plucked up his courage and asked to have his phone back. Olivier bent down to give him the full benefit of his impenetrable sunglasses. "You're lucky to get your car back," he said, slapping the roof.

Rocca drove off, wilting with relief.

CHAPTER TEN

Reboul was pacing across the terrace, anxious for news. He listened intently as Sam gave him a précis.

Thanks to his driver's license, they knew Rocca's name as well as his reluctantly given address. But they were convinced that he knew very little apart from the name of the man who had hired him, which was probably as false as the cover story. As for his description, it could apply to almost any man wearing a Panama hat, white shirt, and sunglasses. All they had to go on was the phone number Rocca had been given and told to use when checking in every evening. There was a name opposite the number in Rocca's phone, but it was a Monsieur Martin, a name shared by more than 220,000 other French families, the equivalent of the Anglo-Saxon Mr. Smith.

Reboul looked and sounded discouraged. "So where do we go from here?"

"Well," said Sam, "we have that number, which is a start. Let's call it, see who answers, and try to get his real name. And I think I know just the person who could do that without raising an alarm: Mimi."

Sam called her to explain the

problem, and his idea — that Mimi pose as someone from the phone company's customer relations department, conducting a survey on customer satisfaction. "If you could get his address as well as his name," said Sam, "that would be great."

Sam could almost hear Mimi shaking her head. "But the phone company would have all that," she said. "Why don't we check with them first?" Which one of Olivier's police pals did, only to find that the subscriber was not a person but a company: Escargot Investments, with a billing address in Monaco.

For a moment, there was a disappointed silence, eventually broken by Sam. "I have an old friend on Wall Street, a researcher for an investment banker. She specializes in corporate secrets. Give her the name of any company, registered anywhere in the world, and she'll find out who owns it." Sam looked around at the others and shrugged. "Or we could go to Monaco and try our luck."

Elena was intrigued by the idea of going to Monaco, which she had never seen, and she asked the obvious question: "Why not do both?"

Activity is the next-best thing to progress, and it was quickly agreed that both was what they would do. First, the call. It was only 7:30 a.m. in New York, but on Wall Street they start early, and Sam's friend picked up after the second ring.

"Gail? It's your old admirer, Sam.

Are you still as beautiful as ever?" He winced, and held the phone away from his ear. "That bad at keeping in touch, am I? I'm sorry, I really am, but I've been traveling a lot. Gail, listen: I'm doing a job in France, and I could use a little information about a company in Monaco." Sam had to endure a few minutes of good-natured scolding from Gail before she calmed down and agreed to see what she could dig up about Escargot Investments in return for lunch — a long lunch — at Daniel next time Sam was in New York.

Sam and Elena set off for Monaco early the next morning. Reboul had insisted that Olivier drive them since he was familiar with Monaco, and said that he had a favorite aunt there he'd be happy to see. As they left Marseille for the autoroute, Elena, always avid for information about any new destination, had her nose deep in a guidebook borrowed from Reboul's library. She shared odd items with Sam: Monaco, covering only 500 acres, could easily fit into New York's Central Park, at nearly 850 acres. The population is about 36,000, made up of more than 120 different nationalities. The first stone of the castle, home of the current prince, was laid on June 10, 1215.

"Morning or afternoon?" said Sam, whose thirst for statistics was limited.

Elena sighed before continuing. "To lure new inhabitants, the early rulers established an attractive fiscal system."

"In other words, residents don't pay taxes. Nice."

The Monaco lecture was tactfully interrupted by Olivier, who asked if they had any plans for lunch. If it was OK with them, he said, he would like to slip away and see his aunt.

Arriving in Monaco, Olivier dropped them off in the Place du Casino, where Sam's attention was caught by one of his favorite French landscapes: the long, shady, inviting terrace of a bar and restaurant. This was the Café de Paris, which Sam at once identified as a perfect spot for lunch. But first, to give them an appetite, he wanted to visit the headquarters of Escargot Investments.

The address supplied by the phone company turned out to be a modern apartment building not far from the casino. Judging by the dozens of discreet brass plaques displayed in the lobby, ordinary residents were vastly outnumbered by companies. And among them, on the fifteenth floor, was Escargot Investments.

The office was marked by yet another brass plaque, fixed to a heavy, locked door. Sam pressed the buzzer, and a metallic voice asked him to identify himself and state his business. "The name is

Phillips," said Sam, "and Herr Trauner, my banker in Zurich, has recommended that I come to see you to discuss an investment project."

The door clicked open, and Elena and Sam found themselves in a small reception area elegantly decorated in shades of gray. A receptionist, equally elegant, was stationed behind a highly polished partners' desk that was bare except for a vase of white roses and an open copy of *Vogue*.

"*Bonjour,*" she said. "I don't believe you have an appointment, do you?"

"That's what I'm here to set up." Sam patted his pockets, and came up with a page torn from his diary.

"Let's see now — I was told to ask for a Monsieur Martin."

The receptionist frowned, disturbing the symmetry of two perfectly plucked eyebrows. "I'm sorry. There's nobody of that name here. Are you sure it wasn't Monsieur Morton?"

Sam slapped his forehead with the palm of his hand. "Of course," he said. "Trust me to get things wrong. Would Monsieur Morton be available for a quick chat?"

The frown deepened, the receptionist apologized again. Monsieur Morton was away on a business trip to Shanghai, and there was no one else available.

"What a bummer," said Sam. "I

don't think we can count that as a great success, do you? Maybe a glass of *rosé* would help."

They were sitting on the terrace of the Café de Paris, looking out across the Place du Casino. Elena, whose fascination for ghoulish details never failed to surprise Sam, was studying the façade of the casino. "Those guys, the heavy gamblers who lose everything at the tables," she said, "where do you think they go to commit suicide?"

"Glad you asked," said Sam. "It's usually under one of those big palm trees over there. If not, the other places should be listed in that little guidebook of yours. Under S."

The wine arrived, and they sat back to enjoy the ever-changing view of the mixed bag of tourists who invade Monaco every summer. As ever, the women's outfits were more stimulating than the endless baseball caps and cargo pants worn by the men, and Sam was enjoying the current fad for short shorts and high heels. Elena was less impressed by another popular summer fashion — white skirts or dresses billowing with layer upon layer of frills that reminded her of her grandma's vintage lampshades. She was elaborating on that theme — "Those dresses are for ten-year-olds with tanned legs" — when Sam's phone rang.

It was Gail, calling from New York, where the time was just past 7 a.m. When Sam complimented her on her early start, she told him that she'd already been to the gym and had had her protein smoothie breakfast.

"OK," she said. "About this Escargot Investments setup. It's complicated, which always makes me think there's some funny business going on. The company's registered in Monaco, but it's owned by a trust in the Cayman Islands, which in turn is owned by an *Anstalt* in Lichtenstein, with branches in Zurich and Nassau. In other words, whoever the real owner is doesn't want the world to know about it."

"But there must be people with names somewhere," said Sam.

"Sure there are — the front men for the trusts, who are usually local

lawyers. That doesn't get us anywhere. I'll keep trying. I have a
friend in Nassau who owes me a
favor. I'll ask him to see what he
can dig up."

"Gail, you're a princess."

"I have just one word for you,
Sam Levitt — Daniel." And with
that, the line went dead.

While Sam had been talking,
Elena had been studying the menu,
nodding her head with evident
satisfaction. "Liver and bacon —
which you never get in the States
anymore — and then *profiteroles*
with hot chocolate sauce," she said.
She closed the menu with a snap,
and leaned forward. "So tell me,
what did your snoop find out?"

A very pleasant hour passed, and

they were having a second cup of coffee when Elena peered over the top of her sunglasses across the Place du Casino. "Well, well, well," she said. "Look who's here, with his favorite aunt." And there, strolling through the crowd, was Olivier, his arm around the waist of an extremely pretty blonde who couldn't have been more than twenty-five.

"I've noticed it before," said Sam. "They do have very young aunts over here. I think it's the Mediterranean climate." He took out his phone and called Olivier. "Could you pick us up in about ten minutes? We're at the Café de Paris." Olivier swung around, saw them, grinned, and gave them the thumbs-up before he and his delightful aunt hurried away through the crowd.

On the drive back to Marseille, Elena dozed and Sam reviewed the progress they'd made. Not much, he had to admit. Not much at all.

CHAPTER ELEVEN

Oleg Vronsky was not a happy man. The only thing he had learned from having Reboul's car followed was that Reboul was aware of it, and more than capable of dealing with it. "So," he said to Nikki, "the man's not a fool, and he knows something is up. I don't know how good his ferrets are, but there's a chance they might find out that I'm involved. That would not please me." Nikki, distracted from the magazine he had been reading,

Body Beautiful, nodded sympatheti-
cally.

They were on board *The Caspian
Queen,* heading east down the
coast toward Cap d'Antibes. Vronsky was to have lunch with Sergei
Kalinin, an old friend from Moscow who had mysterious but clearly
very lucrative connections with the
ministry in charge of exploiting
Russia's natural gas. He, like several
of his well-heeled compatriots, had
decided that a large villa on Cap
d'Antibes was in every way more
attractive than a dacha in the dank
and gloomy forests outside Moscow
or even a palatial beach hut in So-
chi. Better food, for one thing, and
a wider choice of girls. It promised
to be an amusing lunch.

But it was unlikely to bring Vronsky any closer to owning Le Pharo, which, he had convinced himself, he *deserved.* He was one of the most successful men in the world, and among the richest. For years he had been able to have exactly what he wanted. And now, all that stood between him and his dream was that stubborn, arrogant, pain-in-the-ass Frenchman.

Nikki had been with Vronsky long enough to have become an expert in reading his moods, and his boss's growing frustration was increasingly obvious. Nikki too had become tired of the inactivity and lack of progress, and had even considered some extreme solutions of his own to the problem. Abduction? A car bomb? Lacing Reboul's whisky with cyanide? But the difficulty, as he had been often reminded, was that Vronsky, once having taken possession of Le Pharo, intended to make it his base. He would be spending a great deal of time in Marseille, and attention from the local police would be most unwelcome. Scandal must be avoided. Whatever happened to Reboul must happen away from the city. But where? And what?

The Caspian Queen cut her engines and drifted to a halt a few hundred yards offshore. One of the Rivas was lowered and made ready for the short trip to the private jetty, where Kalinin, a barrel of a man wearing camouflage shorts, an I ♡ Putin T-shirt, and a yachting cap, was waiting to greet his guests.

"Oli!"

"Sergei! It's been so long!"

"Too long!"

The two men hugged in the enthusiastic Russian manner, for all the world like two wrestlers, each searching for the opportunity to administer a lethal cross-buttock throw. And then, still grasping one another by the shoulders, they pulled back for the ritual exchange of insults.

Vronsky to the portly Kalinin: "Oy! — I see the diet didn't work."

Kalinin to the shorter Vronsky: "What's this? You've given up wearing those high heels?"

There was a flurry of back-slapping, Nikki was introduced, and the three men went up through a path lined with parasol pines to what Kalinin described as his "little country cottage."

In fact, it was a mansion, built in the 1930s, the stucco faded to the color of a dusty pink. "Once Nabokov was the only Russian living here," said Kalinin. "Now we're all over the place. Vladimir — remember him? — has a villa just up the road, and the Oblomov boys are taking care of the house opposite. They're coming to lunch. Vladimir has a sweet little operation in Nice — you should see his girls! — and the Oblomovs are getting cozy with the Corsican mafia. So it's business as usual. Now, what are you having? I can recommend the '96 Dom Pérignon to settle the dust."

Lunch continued in this jovial fashion, with Champagne, blinis, caviar, and lobster, bikini-clad girls drifting in from the pool, and a burst of Russian song from Kalinin with the coffee. But Vronsky, while enjoying himself, had become somewhat preoccupied. Mention of the Corsican mafia had set him thinking.

On the trip back to *The Caspian Queen* after lunch, the Riva carried two extra passengers: Sasha Oblomov and Igor, his second cousin. Although only distantly related, a shared fondness for violent crime and large amounts of money had brought them closer while they were still young, and they had been working together ever since. Now, at Vronsky's invitation, they had agreed to come on board to discuss what Vronsky described to them as "an interesting project."

The four of them settled into their seats on opposite sides of a low table in Vronsky's personal state-room while a steward bustled about taking orders for cigars and Armagnac. The dress code was clearly flexible — Vronsky in well-pressed linen, Nikki in white jeans and a black muscle shirt, and the Oblomovs looking like two rumpled bears, identically dressed in wrinkled T-shirts and the camouflage shorts that seemed to be *de rigueur* for Russian residents of Cap d'Antibes.

Vronsky waited for the steward to leave before opening the discussion. "I have a problem in Marseille," he said, "and our good friend Sergei suggested that you might be able to help." He studied the glowing tip of his cigar carefully, as though looking for inspiration. "I hope he wasn't being indiscreet, but he did mention that you have — how shall I put it? — business connections in Corsica." He looked at the Oblomovs, eyebrows raised and questioning. They shrugged in unison, a reaction that Vronsky chose to take as confirmation. He continued, under their intent, unblinking eyes, until he had explained his problem and its possible solution, but only in general terms. Details could come later.

Leaning back in his chair, he relit his cigar. "Any questions?"

Sasha Oblomov raised his right hand, palm upward, toward Vronsky and rubbed his thumb across his index finger, the universal shorthand for money. Vronsky smiled. "Good," he said. "Now we can talk."

Francis Reboul was regaining his spirits after the worry and irritation caused by Vronsky's behavior. A couple of days had passed without incident, and without any sign of his being followed. Life seemed to have returned to normal, with Elena and Sam's hunt for an apartment a pleasant distraction.

The blessed relief came to an end over drinks that evening, when Sam broke the news that he had heard back from his spy on Wall Street. "Gail just called," he said. "I don't know how she did it, but she managed to cut through all the offshore crap and fake trusts, and now we know who owns Escargot Investments." He took a deep breath. "I'm afraid, as we suspected, that it's Vronsky. Which means, I guess, that it was probably him who had you followed."

Sam saw Reboul's face tighten, the lines on either side of his mouth becoming deeper and more prominent, his face a mask of anger. Pulling himself together with a visible effort, he said, "I'd like to go through everything that's happened, right from the beginning." He looked at his watch, and swore. "I have an appointment this evening. Sam, could we talk first thing tomorrow?"

The morning saw Reboul still tense, a tension mixed with anger that only grew as he and Sam went over the events of the past few days, from the strafing by helicopter to Vronsky's performance at the charity dinner, his appearance the following day in Reboul's driveway, and his likely involvement in having Reboul's car followed. Sam made an effort to put the situation into perspective.

"Look, he's at best a goddam nuisance and at worst a dangerous weirdo, but he hasn't broken any laws. All the police can do is keep an eye on him from a distance."

Reboul paced up and down, fists clenched. "I've had enough," he said. "I want to have it out with him, tell him to his face that if he doesn't leave me alone there will be consequences."

Sam shook his head. "Sorry, Francis, but that's a lousy idea. All you'll do is make him more determined. I've met guys like him before, and they don't give up easily. Also, don't forget that at least three people who got in his way died in pretty suspicious circumstances."

Sam went over to Reboul and put an arm around his friend's shoulders. "Believe me, this isn't the time to jump in and hope for the best. You know," Sam went on, "at the moment, Vronsky knows more about you than you know about him. It might be useful, for instance, if we knew how long he plans to stay in Marseille. Judging by his record, he's probably less of a problem when he's close than when he's away. What do you think?"

"Sure. The more you know about your enemy the better. But we can hardly call him up and ask him."

"Well," said Sam, "I know someone who can. Our favorite journalist."

CHAPTER TWELVE

"Philippe?"

"Who is this? What time is it?"

"Time for Marseille's top reporter to be out reporting. It's Sam."

"Oh." There was a grunt as Philippe sat up. "Is this urgent?"

"Better than that. It's your chance to do a good deed to help your friend Francis."

"What's he done?"

"It's not him, it's Vronsky. We're pretty sure he's having Francis followed, and God knows what he's

going to try next. We really need to
know more about him. Tell me —
has he ever come back to you about
his invitation to do an interview on
his boat?"

"No. He said he'd call, but he
hasn't."

"Well, I have an idea that he
might fall for."

"I'm listening." Philippe's voice
had changed from drowsy to alert.

"It's something to appeal to his
vanity, and a chance to become
better known in Marseille — which
is one of his social ambitions.
Here's the plot. You have sold your
editorial board on a series of in-
depth profiles of Les Amis de
Marseille, and who better to start
with than the most generous *ami*

of them all, Monsieur Vronsky."

"But I already did him, remember? After the auction."

"Ah," said Sam, "but that was a mere sketch. I'm thinking of a complete portrait: the man in full — his hopes, his dreams, his indiscretions, everything. You know how these rich guys are. They've all got egos the size of a house, they love talking about themselves, and the big plus is that he liked the piece you did on him."

Before there was time for an answer, Sam slipped in the bribe. Knowing Philippe's fondness for lunch in general and Le Bistrot d'Edouard in particular, he suggested that they meet later at the restaurant, where they could dis-

cuss the matter face-to-face. Philippe bowed to the irresistible logic
of Sam's argument. Lunch it was.

Sam put down his phone and
looked across the breakfast table at
Elena. She was bent over the *International New York Times,* her coffee
and croissant forgotten, her face
intent and frowning. This, as Sam
had come to know all too well, was
her Do Not Disturb look. She finished the piece she was reading,
gave a dismissive snort, and pushed
the paper away with the back of her
hand.

"God, they make me sick, those
deadbeats in Washington," she said.
"The sooner they're kicked out and
replaced by women the better."
Warming to her subject, she

wagged an outraged finger at Sam. "How can you be anti-abortion and pro-gun? These idiots drone on about the sanctity of human life — even though the human hasn't even been born — and yet they and their buddies at the NRA choose to ignore the fact that guns kill thousands of Americans every year. Does that make sense?"

Elena left Sam to ponder this interesting question while she attacked her croissant. In fact, he had for many years been immune from the charms of any politician, regardless of party, and he was still surprised that anyone could take a bunch of such self-serving windbags seriously. It was a point of view that Elena considered constitutionally irresponsible, and so he decided to drop the subject and move on to safer ground.

"How would you like to come to lunch with two admirers?" he said. "Philippe and me."

Elena looked up at him and smiled, her mood suddenly sunny. "I think I could make myself available."

It was a couple of years since Philippe had introduced Elena and Sam to Chez Edouard, and it had been, for both of them, love at first bite. Elena could still remember what she had eaten, and was tempted to have the same again. *Tapas* in all their glory, from *pata negra* ham to tuna roe with a drizzle of olive oil, fried aubergine dusted with mint, tartare of salmon with honey and dill, deep-fried zucchini flowers, artichokes, anchovies, clams — there were fifteen dishes in all, and, as Elena said, she could happily try each one. But, with a small gesture to moderation, they eventually settled on four *tapas* each, with sharing privileges.

There is a special moment in a good restaurant that comes before eating a single mouthful, and it should be listed at the top of the menu. It is anticipation, in the sure and certain knowledge that you won't be disappointed. Your order has been taken, your first glass of wine is to hand, tantalizing whiffs come through the kitchen door each time it swings open, waiters scurry, there is the moist creak of corks being eased out of bottles, and everything is as it should be. You settle back in your seat, and all's well with the world. "Heaven," said Elena.

Philippe had reserved a table in the upstairs dining room, with its hand-lettered frieze repeated around the room urging everyone to *buvez, riez, chantez* — drink, laugh, sing. It was still a little early for the singing, but the other two suggestions were being followed with great enthusiasm.

"Now," said Sam, "this is a working lunch, OK? Let's start with what we know, and then we can figure out what to do. First, we know that Vronsky badly wants Le Pharo. Second, we know that he has a record of getting what he wants, often by arranging for obstacles, even human obstacles, to disappear. Third, he's always somewhere else when anything messy happens. That's about it, and it's not enough." He paused to sample his wine. "Every man has his weakness, something that makes him vulnerable, and that's what I'd love to find out." He nodded toward Philippe. "And our best chance of doing that is you."

Before Philippe had time to reply, the *tapas* arrived, an entire landscape of *tapas* that took up most of the table, and thoughts of Vronsky were put aside while due respect was paid to the chef.

"That was perfect," said Elena, as she wiped the final traces of honey and dill from her plate with a scrap of bread. "I'm so glad we didn't order a main course. Did you see they have *churros* and chocolate sauce for dessert?"

It was Sam's turn to roll his eyes. How Elena ate what she ate without any visible weight gain was a mystery to him. "Let's get back to it. Philippe, what do you think? You must have interviewed a few captains of industry in your time. They like to talk, don't they?"

"Try to stop them." Philippe took a long pull at his wine. "As long as you stick to their favorite subject."

"Which is themselves, right?"

"Right. Getting him to talk shouldn't be difficult."

Elena put her hand on Philippe's arm. "We must do something," she said. "All this is getting to Francis. I hate to see him so worried."

Philippe nodded. "Let me work on it. For me, it depends on how much he wants to be a big shot in Marseille. If he does — and I think he does — we shouldn't have a problem."

Elena squeezed his arm. "For that, you can have one of my *churros.*"

Sam raised his glass to Philippe. "Over to you, *jeune homme.*"

Meanwhile, the phone lines between Cap d'Antibes and Corsica had been busy, with the Oblomovs putting out feelers among their contacts in Calvi and Ajaccio. But in such a small and tight-knit community it was almost impossible for even a single feeler to go unnoticed, particularly where murder and money were concerned. Ears were always cocked for careless remarks, and it wasn't long before hints that there was something in the wind reached Flo and Jo, the Figatelli brothers.

Moving as they frequently did in some of the less conventional circles of Corsican society, they often heard gossip and news that were not for public consumption, and so it was this time. Their friend and occasional business colleague

Maurice, a professional barfly, had overheard snatches of a conversation which suggested that some Riviera Russians were offering a truckload of money to make someone disappear. The Figatellis, ever alert to rumors of this sort, asked Maurice to continue his researches and report back, with a bonus if he could identify the target.

The Oblomovs were beginning to feel quite at home on *The Caspian Queen.* Once again they were in the luxurious cocoon of Vronsky's stateroom, cigars and cognac to hand, to present a progress report. It started on an encouraging note.

"You tell us you want good news," said Sasha Oblomov. "We bring you good news. There is a man in Calvi, Nino Zonza, who we have worked with on one or two projects. He says he can help us."

"In what way?" asked Vronsky.

"In every way." Oblomov took a swig of cognac and shuddered with pleasure. "He'll even arrange the burial, if that's what you want."

Vronsky nodded his approval. He liked dealing with full-service professionals. "But don't forget," he said, "there must be no possibility of my being implicated."

"Zonza can guarantee that, as long as the job is done in Corsica." He leaned forward, tapping the side of his nose with an index finger. "Where certain things can be arranged without bothering the

French authorities."

"Now," said Vronsky, "what would induce Reboul to take a trip to Corsica? Think about that. Meanwhile, we need to find out more about him — not just his movements, but his habits. And this time, I don't want any amateurs chasing after his car. So find me someone serious."

Oblomov scratched the stubble on his skull. "Let's see — we want someone with the experience and the contacts to uncover all the nasty little details." His expression brightened. "Someone, for instance, like my divorce lawyer in Nice. He has informers all along the coast, and he found out stuff about my ex-wife she even didn't know. And he keeps his mouth shut."

Vronsky, a survivor of uncomfortably thorough divorce proceedings himself, liked the idea. And so investigations were set in place by both sides, with neither side being aware of being investigated.

CHAPTER THIRTEEN

Vronsky had been pleased and even
a little flattered to receive Philippe's
invitation to be the first subject in
an important series of interviews.
He felt at ease with the young
journalist, and he saw this as an opportunity to establish himself as
one of the more important benefac-
tors of what he now thought of as
his adopted city. And so he was
happy to agree that the first session
should take place on board *The
Caspian Queen,* where, inciden-

tally, his toys and his retinue would be on display.

For Philippe, the interview began in promising fashion with a short but luxurious trip in a chauffeur-driven Riva. His host was waiting to greet him at the top of the gang-plank, wreathed in welcoming smiles, and Philippe recognized at once that he was going to be given the treatment. There would be flattery and ego massage, and Vronsky would behave as though this was the high spot of his day. Philippe had seen it all many times before, usually from minor public officials hoping that a favorable interview would propel them into the giddy heights of becoming major public officials. But, familiar though he was with the routine, Philippe had to admit that Vronsky was starting to put on an impressive performance.

The first act was a short guided tour of the more obvious attractions of a simple life at sea — the Rivas, the helicopters, the freshwater pool (Vronsky had found that salt water made him itch), the sundeck, the cocktail deck, and the bridge, with its battery of the latest electronic marvels. Philippe did his best to appear impressed by it all, although his overriding impression, which of course he kept to himself, was that the money spent on this floating extravagance would have been far better spent buying a magnificent house in Marseille, an apartment in Paris, and two or three choice vineyards in Cassis.

Moving inside, Philippe was taken through the vast sitting room and into the guest quarters: five suites, each with its own jacuzzi and, as Vronsky said with a modest smile, each with its own sea view. From there, they inspected a kitchen that would have made a three-star chef feel at home, a wine cellar fit for a château, and a cold room with separate sections devoted to foie gras and caviar. As Vronsky said, it was little details like this that made *The Caspian Queen* such a comfortable home away from home.

"And, if I may ask, where is home?" said Philippe.

"The world," said Vronsky. "The

world is my home. Now let me show you my office, and then we can get down to work."

The office was large and modern, decorated with tributes to Oleg Vronsky. The enormous head of a bear shot in Siberia shared space on one wall with a giant black-and-white photograph of Vronsky, in tails, whirling around a ballroom with a pretty girl in his arms. Other, smaller photographs showed Vronsky with various celebrities of the kind that rich men attract, and there were several framed letters, most of them in Russian, that Vronsky described as coming from "friends in high places."

Champagne was served, and cigars were offered. Philippe took out his list of questions and a tape recorder, and the interview began.

A couple of hours away, in a smaller and less elaborate office just off the Promenade des Anglais in Nice, the divorce lawyer Antoine Prat was bent over a notepad, toying with zeros, trying to estimate how much his latest assignment might be worth. His most recent client, Sasha Oblomov, had instructed him to spare nothing in his efforts to uncover every detail of Francis Reboul's life and movements. The investigation would be long and complex and, if Prat had anything to do with it, ferociously expensive. He congratulated himself, as he frequently did, on having chosen an occupation that feeds off human weakness, fallibility, and greed, three qualities that had helped to reward him so generously over the years. Tucking his scribbled calculations away in a drawer, he summoned his secretary, the nubile Nicole, and started to plan his first steps.

That evening, Reboul had decided to put aside the cares of the day and introduce Elena to one of his favorite Provençal wines, the pale and elegant *rosé* of Château la Canorgue, a *vin bio* made without the addition of extra sulfites. This, so Reboul claimed, made the wine not only delicious but also good for you, a theory that Elena was testing with enthusiasm. She was delighted that Reboul seemed more like his old lighthearted self; she had become very fond of him, and she was quick to encourage any distraction, liquid or otherwise, that might cheer him up.

The first glass was going down surprisingly quickly, as first glasses often do. "It's working," said Elena. "I'm feeling better already." Reboul smiled, topped up her glass, and was about to explain the connection between sulfites and hangovers when Sam joined them, exchanging the phone in his hand for a glass as he sat down.

"That was Philippe," he said, "who has just had his ass kissed from one end of Vronsky's boat to the other."

Reboul winced at the thought. "So I gather it went well."

"It could hardly have gone better. If Vronsky hadn't had a dinner date, Philippe would still be on the boat."

"Did he get anything interesting?" asked Elena.

"Nothing dramatic," said Sam. "It's probably too soon to expect any of the indiscreet stuff. But Vronsky wants another session, this time with a photographer, so it looks promising."

Reboul put down his glass and leaned forward. "Look," he said, "Vronsky wants Le Pharo — God knows he's made that obvious enough. And if what we hear is true, he'll do whatever it takes to get it. But what is that, and how does he plan to do it? I'm sorry, but he's not going to tell a journalist, is he?"

Sam held up his hand. "You can never tell what he might let slip. Once he gets really comfortable with Philippe — and it seems to be headed in that direction — he'll let his guard down. He'll start saying things to show how smart he is. It happens all the time. Besides, at the moment, Philippe is our only contact with Vronsky. I know it's frustrating, but I think our best bet is to be patient and wait for him to make his move. And, while we're waiting, to be careful. Very careful."

Over dinner, at Sam's suggestion,

they started to put together a list of subjects and questions for Philippe to put to Vronsky during the next session. Patience, however, was going to be difficult.

CHAPTER FOURTEEN

It was a fine soft Corsican evening, and the Figatelli brothers were waiting, as agreed, outside the entrance to their bar in Calvi, not far from the site of the house where Christopher Columbus was born. It had been several days before they had managed to secure an audience with the man they were about to see, and they had only succeeded in this because of a small service they had been able to carry out for him the previous year. They had suggested meeting in the back room of the bar. But their contact, a cautious man, preferred to avoid the risk of being seen with them in public. He would send a car to pick them up and take them somewhere more discreet.

With a punctuality rare in Corsica, a big gray Renault pulled up precisely on time. It was driven by a man who, at first sight, seemed to have no neck — just a massive head growing out of even more massive shoulders. He motioned with a jerk of the head for the Figatellis to get into the car, and then he set off, ignoring their attempts to make conversation. A few minutes later, he pulled up outside a weather-stained, ancient house in the old quarter of town. The front door was opened by another giant, his size accentuated by a close-fitting T-shirt. He led the Figatellis down an ill-lit passageway and into a cavernous, darkened room with a high, vaulted ceiling. The only sign of life was the muted glow from the screen of a television, its sound turned down.

This was the headquarters of Nino Zonza, a man who, for fifty years, had been an influential, if little-known, figure behind the scenes of the Corsican underworld. Those who did know him valued him highly for his network of sources, and for the extent and accuracy of his information. Local legend had it that if you scratched your backside in Ajaccio, the news would have reached Zonza in Calvi within an hour.

"Come in. Sit down." The voice coming from the back of the room was thin but husky. Their host, a tiny, hairless man withered by the passage of time, was perched on the edge of an armchair several sizes too big for him. He peered at the Figatelli brothers through dense black sunglasses.

"I remember you two boys," he said. "You were useful. What do you want from an old man like me?"

"It's a pleasure to see you again, Monsieur Zonza," said Jo. "And we would very much appreciate your help." Zonza inclined his head, his sunglasses reflecting the glow from the TV screen. Jo continued. "We've heard a rumor. It seems that some Russians from the Riviera are making inquiries in connection with a certain job they would like done. A disappearance."

"Ah yes," said the old man. "One hears rumors like that more and more these days." He smiled, and shook his head. "It's a dangerous old world."

Jo smiled back. "It certainly is. Now, there is talk of a prominent Marseille businessman somehow involved. And, as we have many friends in Marseille, we would like to know who that might be." Jo spread his hands and shrugged. "In case we could help."

"Indeed," said Zonza. "I can understand your interest. But information such as this — so delicate, so secret — is never easy to come by. And naturally, it is never given away."

"Of course, of course. But we would be happy to . . ."

Zonza held up an age-speckled hand. "There will be time enough to discuss payment if the information should become available. Let me think about it. If I should hear anything, I shall have a message left for you at your bar."

"Do you know the address?" asked Jo.

Zonza smiled, revealing numerous gold teeth. "I know everything about Calvi."

Once the Figatellis had been shown out, Zonza poured himself a glass of *myrte* and considered his position. The previous week, he had been asked to consider an attractive offer from the Oblomovs. Now it seemed that the Figatellis were becoming involved, and, being Corsican himself, he would much prefer to do business with Corsicans; that is, of course, providing they would be prepared to match the Russian offer. But, he told himself, there was no need to rush to a decision. In fact, it might be possible to string both sides along, taking payments from each of them. Interesting. He poured himself a second glass of *myrte,* turned up the sound on the television, and settled back to watch the rerun of another episode of *Dallas*.

The Figatellis, sitting over coffee in the back room of their bar, compared their impressions of the meeting.

"Well," said Flo, "am I getting suspicious in my old age or does he know a lot more than he let on?"

"He must know all about it. If Maurice was able to pick up the rumor during a sober moment, Zonza, with that network of his, would certainly have heard. How many people does he have out on the street with their ears flapping? A dozen? Fifty? He must know."

The brothers sat in silence for a few moments, trying to think of some way to induce Zonza to tell them what he had learned. But, as they had to admit, he was not a man who would respond kindly to pressure. Threats were out of the question. Money might work, but how much would it take?

"If we could find out who these Russians are, we'd at least have some options," said Jo. He took out his phone. "Let's get Maurice over here. Maybe he can remember where he got his information."

Maurice made his entrance in his usual furtive fashion, as though he were half-expecting to be mugged. Small and dark, with a scruffy little beard, he prided himself on his unremarkable appearance. "It's easy to get lost in a crowd," he was fond of saying, "but I can almost vanish in an empty room." And it was true. Like a chameleon, he was able to blend in with his surroundings. It was an eavesdropper's greatest asset.

He accepted a glass of Corsican whisky and looked at the Figatellis expectantly, the possibility of another job never far from his thoughts.

"Remember that rumor you heard?" asked Flo. "About a couple of Russians?"

Maurice held up both hands. "Don't rush me. I've got the word out, but these things aren't on the evening news. Finding the name of the target? That's going to take time."

"Maybe it would be easier if we knew the names of the Russians."

"Ah." Maurice scratched his beard. "You're right. One thing leads to another. Do you want me to . . ."

Flo grinned. "That little bonus of yours is getting bigger all the time."

Maurice finished his whisky and stood up. "Always a pleasure, gentlemen. I'll get back to you."

CHAPTER FIFTEEN

The first Vronsky interview, with Philippe employing the slavish flattery he would normally reserve for insecure politicians, had gone well. By the time it had finished, Vronsky seemed relaxed, comfortable, and, so Philippe hoped, more likely to let slip an indiscretion or two. For this next session, Vronsky had even agreed to leave the floating womb of *The Caspian Queen* and meet Philippe for lunch at Peron, only insisting that a separate table for one be reserved for Nikki, the ever-present bodyguard.

Lunch started with a reaction from Vronsky that boded well for the interview. This was his first visit to Peron, and he was delighted with the expansive sea view, which happened to feature *The Caspian Queen* at anchor five hundred yards away.

"You see?" he said, nodding at the yacht. "She follows me like a faithful dog."

Philippe smiled and poured the wine. "I've been thinking," he said. "You've had a fascinating life, been all over the world, made millions — excuse me, billions — and it would be a great shame if we tried to compress all that you've achieved into this one article. It cries out for more important treatment."

Vronsky's eyebrows went up. "You have something in mind?"

"I do. I'd like to suggest that I write your biography."

Philippe was expecting a reaction — an attack of false modesty, perhaps, or a little preening, but Vronsky said nothing while he turned the idea over in his mind. Like so many rich and successful men, he was often the target of a nagging feeling that whatever he had wasn't quite enough. Something was lacking. Recognition, fame, celebrity — however it was described, it would be the ultimate public confirmation that he, Oleg Vronsky, was exceptional. And a flattering biography was one way of achieving that. Not surprisingly, Vronsky found the idea appealing.

"I've done a little research," said Philippe, "and it's a great rags-to-riches story: modest beginnings, risk and adventure in Africa and Brazil, enormous success — people will love it." He shook his head. "I'm sorry. I know we're here to work on the interview. But I'm really excited about the biography. Would you think about it?"

With the seed planted, Philippe went back to his notes, and the questions began. They started harmlessly enough: How did Vronsky like France? What would be his next stop after Marseille? Did he play golf? Where did he stay when he was in London or Paris? Did he spend any time on the Riviera?

This led naturally into Philippe's next question. "I've heard," he said, "that dozens of Russians have settled in the South of France. Do you know many of them?"

"A few," said Vronsky, "but not here. It's too quiet for them here — not enough parties. They prefer the Riviera. Cap d'Antibes, for instance. I was there not long ago, and it's getting to be like a suburb of Moscow."

As lunch continued and the wine flowed, Vronsky revealed that he had little time for his countrymen: "Peasants, for the most part, peasants who have struck it lucky — loud, vulgar, and uncultured." Philippe, feeling that the protestations were a little too glib, wasn't altogether convinced. He made a mental note to look into the Russian colony on the coast.

As lunch drew to its liquid end, Philippe told Vronsky that he had enough material to start writing, and promised to arrange for a photographer to come and take pictures of the great man on his yacht, and perhaps at the wheel of his Bentley. They parted company on the best of terms, each feeling that the meeting had been more than satisfactory.

Nino Zonza was experiencing an unusual moment of indecision. Normally a man who made up his mind quickly, he found himself torn between the lucrative deal he had made with the Oblomovs and his natural instinct to side with the Figatellis, who were, like him, good Corsicans.

To add to his difficulties, there was the problem of what to do with the losers. If he should decide in favor of the Figatellis, the Oblomovs would be sure to look for revenge. And if he should choose the Oblomovs? Well, Calvi is a small town, and there are precious few secrets. The Figatellis would undoubtedly find out that he had taken a decision against them. They would be displeased, and a displeased Corsican on your doorstep is a very dangerous man.

Eventually, it was this consideration that helped him reach a solution that he found satisfactory: give the winners the problem, and let them take care of the losers. Yes. That would do very well. He summoned his chauffeur and gave him a scribbled note to be delivered to the Figatellis' bar in the Rue de la Place.

The meeting was set for the following evening. As before, the Figatellis were picked up near the Citadelle and deposited at Zonza's house by the mute chauffeur. But this time, the old man showed signs of hospitality, with a tray, three glasses, and a bottle of *myrte* on the low table in front of his armchair when his guests arrived. He waved the brothers to sit down opposite him.

"As I put in my note," he said, "certain information has come my way that may be of interest to you. I shall be more specific, but first" — he smiled his gold-tooth smile — "perhaps you would care for some refreshment." He filled the three glasses, holding the bottle with both hands to compensate for the tremors of old age.

He raised his glass. "To you, my fellow Corsicans." They sipped the peppery, sweet liquid. Zonza dabbed his lips with a silk handkerchief, settled back in his chair, and began to speak.

The call came through later that

evening, as Reboul was stepping out of the shower. By the time it had finished, he had dripped dry. He dressed quickly, and went downstairs to find Sam having a glass of wine with Elena before dinner. Ignoring them, he went straight to the bar and poured himself a large brandy.

"Francis, you look as if you've seen a ghost." Sam went over and patted his friend on the shoulder. "What's the matter?"

Reboul took a long swig of brandy before answering, and Sam noticed that the hand holding the glass was trembling. "I've just had a call from Jo Figatelli in Calvi." Another swig of brandy. "There's a contract out to have me killed."

"What?"

"Jo says it's being set up by two *voyous* — Russians, both of them — and that can't be a coincidence; it's got to be that bastard Vronsky. He's behind it, I'm sure."

Elena and Sam watched as Reboul drained his glass and went back for more. "Is this real?" asked Sam. "Not just a rumor from a bar?"

Reboul shook his head. "Jo's smarter than that. And besides, he got this from an old crook called Zonza, who runs most of the crime in Calvi. He's been approached by these two Russians, the Oblomovs, who are looking for some local help to carry out the contract with them. They've promised Zonza a lot of money if he can find a couple of reliable men — Corsicans, obviously — to work with them setting things up. That's not a problem, but there's a complication: part of the deal is that the job must be done in Corsica, and not mainland France."

"Why?" asked Elena, and then the penny dropped. "Oh, I get it. If it is Vronsky, he won't be anywhere near Corsica when the job's done. That's his usual alibi, isn't it? He'll be a long way away, and he'll have witnesses to prove it. Clean hands, no worries."

Reboul had started to look a little better. Shock had been replaced by anger, and he was seething with outrage. "What can we do to get

234

rid of this lunatic?"

"Well," said Sam, "without some hard evidence, it's no good going to the police, and so far he's covered his tracks pretty well. Short of blowing up his boat or bribing his bodyguard to dump him overboard, it's not easy to see how to get at him. But we'll find a way. There's always a way." And, as the evening wore on, Sam came up with a suggestion that they all agreed had possibilities.

"This is a long shot," he said. "But if we could catch the Oblomovs red-handed, that would give us some serious pressure to put on them. If their choices were a bullet in the head, a lifetime in jail, or co-operation, they might be persuaded to turn state's evidence, spill the beans on Vronsky, and leave him facing a charge of conspiracy to commit murder. That should be enough to put him away for a very long time, safe and sound in a Marseille prison. The big problem, of course, is catching them red-handed, and that particular trap needs to be baited."

Sam paused, and turned to Reboul. "In other words, the Oblomovs need to know you're in Corsica before they'll make their move."

It was getting late, and it wasn't a decision to be taken lightly. They agreed to sleep on it, but before going to bed Sam made a quick call to Philippe.

■ ■ ■ ■

The next morning was gray and drizzly, rare for Marseille, and the weather matched the somber expressions of the group having breakfast while waiting for Philippe. Reboul looked haggard after a night with little sleep, and it took large doses of coffee and sympathy from Elena and Sam to lift his spirits.

Philippe arrived, wet and concerned. Sam's call had given him the bare bones of the bad news, but no details. "Tell me everything," he said, and Reboul repeated the conversation of the previous night, with Philippe shaking his head in disbelief. "This is crazy," he said.

"Are you sure it's true?"

"Jo's a good man. He doesn't scare easily and he doesn't make things up. I believe him."

"And you think Vronsky would do this just because you won't sell him your house?"

Reboul leaned forward, tapping the table for emphasis. "He has a history, remember? His partner in Africa? His partner in Russia? A business contact in New York? All dead. That's his solution for dealing with people who get in his way. Vronsky has no rules. He thinks he can do anything he wants, and so far he's been right. Why should it be any different this time? So yes, I do believe Jo."

There was silence around the

table until Reboul left his seat and started pacing up and down. "I've had enough," he said. "I've never in my life run away from problems, and I'm not going to start now." He stopped in front of Sam. "Call Jo, and work out a plan with him. I'm going to Corsica."

CHAPTER SIXTEEN

The Figatelli brothers stood at the entrance to their bar, consulting their watches as the early evening parade of tourists strolled up and down the Rue de la Place. In the small room behind the bar that served as an office, a bottle of Clos Capitoro, a fine red wine from Porticcio, had been opened and left to breathe. Sam had just called from Sainte-Catherine, the local airport; he'd landed, he was on his way, and the Figatellis were impatient to see him. If past experience was anything to go by, there was never a dull moment when Sam had one of his ideas.

A taxi pulled up outside the bar and the Figatellis took up their positions on either side of the entrance. The elaborate salutes they performed as Sam left the taxi turned into enthusiastic hugs before they went through the bar and into their office.

"Well, my friends," said Sam, "this is just like old times. Do you want to start, or shall I?" He accepted the glass of wine that Flo gave him and took a thoughtful sip. "Mmm. I could get to like this."

"Made it myself," said Flo. "We have some news, but why don't you start? How's Francis?"

"He's OK, but he's pretty mad at Vronsky. And he's hell-bent on coming to Corsica. He's even worked out a reason to come. Did you know he has an aunt who lives here? She has a house in a village called Speloncato, and he's putting out a story that she's getting over an operation, and he wants to check that she's getting proper care. I'm not happy about him being here, but we'll talk about that later. If he really does come, we need to work out a way to keep him safe."

"Here's something that might help," said Jo. "When we were with Zonza, we asked him for the names of the two guys he lined up to help the Oblomovs. They're local boys, and we have friends who know them. So, there are a couple of interesting possibilities." He paused to refill their glasses. "First, we might be able to persuade these two guys to change sides, and tell us what the Oblomovs plan to do about Francis — how they're going to do the job and when. And second, if we have that information, we could use it to ambush the Oblomovs before they have a chance to do anything dangerous."

"That's great, and it's certainly a help," said Sam, "but don't forget this is all about nailing Vronsky. We need to have proof that he set it up. We need confessions from the Oblomovs."

The plotting continued well into

the bottle of wine, and then over dinner. By the time Sam left the following morning, a plan had been agreed, with only one final detail left to be resolved: a way of letting the Oblomovs know, without causing suspicion, when and where Reboul's visit would take place. But the Figatellis had no doubt that Zonza could be used to pass the information on.

Sam, reviewing the plan during the fifty-five-minute flight back to Marseille, felt that it had been a very worthwhile trip.

Patience had never been one of Oleg Vronsky's virtues, and, now that the decision had been made to dispose of Reboul, he was becoming increasingly anxious to make progress. The regular calls from one of the Oblomovs, always in the evening, had so far ended in disappointment. The same problem — how they were to get Reboul over to Corsica — was the subject of daily discussion. Plans had been made, examined, discarded. It was all very frustrating.

And so when Sasha Oblomov broke the pattern and called in the morning, Vronsky had a feeling that his luck might have changed.

"You have news?" he asked.

"The best," said Oblomov. "My contact in Calvi just called. He told me that Reboul is coming over to Corsica for a couple of days next week. There is some old aunt he wants to see. And this is where it gets really interesting. She lives in a village called Speloncato — not too far from Calvi, but remote, surrounded by wild country. It sounds perfect. We can get him going in or coming out."

"Good. Very good. Call me when you've worked out a plan."

In high good humor, Vronsky called Philippe to explain that the photographic session arranged for the following week would have to be postponed. An urgent business problem required Vronsky's presence in Paris. Philippe was the soul of understanding, and wished him a successful trip. All that remained for Vronsky to do was to ask his secretary to reserve his usual suite in the Bristol, *et voilà.* His alibi would be established.

Philippe's journalistic experience had made him suspicious of evasive action taken by his interview subjects at the next-to-last moment, and, smelling a Russian rat, he called Sam.

"It's happened to me a few times before," Philippe said. "Usually politicians who have just been caught with their pants down and don't need any more publicity. This time, I don't know."

"I do," said Sam. "It means they're getting ready to make a move. Can you get away from work early so we can talk to Francis?"

When Philippe arrived at the end of the afternoon, he found Reboul surprisingly relaxed for a man whose life was under threat, opening a bottle of Champagne before the three of them settled down to business.

"I'll be fine," he said. "I have you two, I have the Figatelli boys and all their contacts, and, most important, we have advance information. We know what they're going to try before they try it. The fact that Vronsky is running off to Paris is proof that he's arranged it all. It's what he's always done — he's never there when accidents happen." He raised his glass. *"Bon voyage!"*

Sam had plans for Reboul, but they could wait until later; he didn't want to dampen his friend's optimistic mood. They had a pleasant half hour before Philippe had to leave to cover one of his less thrilling assignments — a cocktail party marking the opening of the new branch of a local bank. "Warm white wine and a lot of back-slapping," he said. "But they're regular advertisers in the paper, so someone has to go." He sighed, finished his Champagne, looked sadly at what remained in the bottle, and left.

"Well, I think I should come too."

"Absolutely not."

Elena and Sam were in their suite, making leisurely preparations before going down to join Reboul for dinner. Elena had suggested that she should accompany Sam and

Reboul to Corsica, an idea that had not found any favor with Sam.

"It's too dangerous."

"Nonsense. There'll be you, Francis, the Figatelli boys, and half the Corsican underworld to hide behind. And besides, I think Francis needs a woman's support. And besides that, I'd like to come."

"Not a chance."

The argument continued until Elena slipped off to the bathroom, only to reappear dressed in the cobwebs of silk that did duty as her underwear.

"Why is it," asked Sam, "that whenever you start losing an argument you take off your clothes? Could that be coincidence?"

"That's not coincidence, baby.

That's tactics. Get your body over here."

The argument was adjourned.

They came down to dinner, a little late and a little flushed, to find Reboul restless, and bubbling with good humor. He had clearly come to terms with the situation, and was confident that Sam and the Figatellis could handle it. And he was finding the whiff of danger rather stimulating. Should he arm himself? he asked Sam. What about a bulletproof vest?

Sam recognized this as a typical first-timer's reaction. There is a heightened awareness, excitement mixed with a squirt of adrenaline, that often accompanies physical risk. And so, to humor Reboul,

Sam decided to give him some advice about preparing for his moment of skullduggery.

"First," he said, "don't shoot until you see the whites of their eyes. Second, if you need to go into what might be a dangerous area, send your chauffeur in first to check it out. Third, never answer your phone when someone's pointing a gun at you."

Reboul was laughing and shaking his head. "OK, OK. I was only asking."

Over dinner, the conversation turned to Vronsky. He, as they had heard from Philippe, was going to be well out of the way in Paris. But they still had to implicate him beyond doubt if they were to succeed in having him convicted and imprisoned.

"Do we know where he's staying in Paris?" asked Reboul.

"Good point," said Sam. "I'll get Philippe to find out. He can say he needs to be in touch to fix another date for the photographic session. And on the subject of Paris, does your police buddy Hervé have some good contacts up there? Vronsky might need to be persuaded not to leave France."

"Of course. I'll call Hervé tomorrow."

Elena was well aware that Sam had no intention of putting Reboul in harm's way, but curiosity was getting the better of her. "These two Russian thugs, the Oblomovs

— what's going to make them agree to blow the whistle on Vronsky?"

"I'm working on it," said Sam. "We've had an idea that might solve the problem, but I'm superstitious. I don't want to talk about it until it's set up."

The idea, hatched between Sam and the Figatellis during their meeting in the back room of the bar, was about to be put to the test. Once again, the brothers were paying a call on Nino Zonza. After the obligatory glass of *myrte* had been sipped and admired, Jo Figatelli opened the proceedings with a question to which he already knew the answer. But he wanted confirmation. "Tell me, Monsieur Nino, these two men you have so quickly found to work with the Oblomovs, are they local?"

Zonza nodded. "Two local boys. Very good, but very expensive. I was shocked." He shrugged. "But one has to pay for quality."

The Figatellis nodded their sympathy in unison. "Terrible, terrible," said Jo. "And have they met the Oblomovs?"

"Not yet. They will be introduced tomorrow, when the Oblomovs arrive in Corsica. Why do you ask?"

"Because we have a proposition that will save you money and make life much easier for us all," said Jo.

Zonza leaned forward, the pleasant thought of saving money adding to his curiosity. "What do you have in mind?" He allowed himself a small joke. "Nothing illegal, I hope?"

"Not at all. Just a little change in personnel. You cancel the boys, so you won't have to pay them."

"And?"

"You use us. We're free."

Zonza's eyebrows went up, and he nodded thoughtfully. "Another glass of *myrte,* gentlemen?"

CHAPTER SEVENTEEN

It was Vronsky's first morning in Paris, and although he was not by nature optimistic — no Russian is, and with good reason — he was beginning to think that fate was on his side.

What could go wrong? Oblomov had just called to say that he and his cousin were taking the evening flight out of Marseille to Calvi. The following morning, they would meet the two local men recruited by Zonza and spend the day with them making detailed preparations. The day after that, Reboul was scheduled to arrive and make his way to his aunt's house in Speloncato, where he planned to stay for two or three days — plenty of time to arrange for his disposal. Again, he thought: What could go wrong? He lit a celebratory cigar and looked at his watch. Natasha had been let loose on the boutiques of the Avenue Montaigne, for which she seemed to have an endless appetite. But even the most hardened shopping addict needs nourishment, and Vronsky had made reservations for lunch at the Cigale Récamier, where the chef did miraculous things with soufflés. It was turning into an excellent day.

For Sam, too, events had taken a very welcome turn. Jo Figatelli had called to say that he and Flo had reached agreement with Zonza to replace the original hired thugs, and they would be meeting the Oblomovs the next day. To Jo's disappointment, Sam had reminded him that the two Russians should not be drowned, mutilated, or even beaten up; it was essential that they be caught in the act. This would allow much more pressure to be put on them to point the finger at Vronsky. Sam and the Figatellis agreed to have one last meeting in Calvi that evening to double-check the details.

Sam, needless to say, had eventually agreed to Elena's coming to

259

Corsica with Reboul, but only on condition that she observe strict safety precautions. There was to be no wandering alone through the streets, no visits to hairdressers or solitary mornings on the beach. At no time was she to be unaccompanied.

On his way to the airport, Sam received another call from Jo, who had just learned that the Oblomovs would be on the same flight to Calvi. "You can't miss them," Jo said. "Zonza told us that they are pretty big and, according to him, very scruffy. He said they looked like two bears in need of a bath."

And when Sam got to the airport, there they were at the check-in desk — large, unkempt, and dressed in camouflage fatigues. A most unsavory pair, with matching bad teeth, muttering to each other in Russian. Their conversation, subdued and confidential, continued as the plane took off and headed for Calvi. They were discussing the relative merits of guns, knives, garrotes, and blunt instruments, all of which, so Zonza had told them, could be made available at a moment's notice. The most important decision, of course, was timing, but Reboul's planned stay of two or three days should give them plenty of opportunity to choose the perfect moment.

Six rows behind them, Sam was considering the next few days, and how Reboul would react when put in the position of human bait.

There were no doubts about his willingness or his bravery, but danger — especially when one isn't used to it — can have unpredictable effects on even the most courageous of men. It was this thought that prompted Sam to take another look at the idea he had briefly considered a couple of days before. But first, there was one crucial question to be answered.

And an hour later, once again in the back room of the Figatellis' bar, it was.

"Are you sure about this?" said Sam. "The Oblomovs have never met Reboul? Never even seen him?"

"No. They're relying on Zonza's hired men — that's Flo and me —

to identify him when he arrives at the airport. Otherwise, all they will have seen are a few blurred shots from the Internet and newspaper clippings, and those don't give any idea of his height or build. So it's our job to point him out."

"Good, very good," said Sam. "Now, we'll need a car with darkened windows and a chauffeur, a wide-brim Panama hat, and big sunglasses, and we'll be all set. I'll talk to Francis when I get back and fill him in." Two puzzled faces looked at him across the table. Jo was the first to speak.

"Fill him in?"

"Sorry — I should have said. I've just decided I'm going to be Francis for a day or two."

After another half hour of detailed discussion, the three of them left the bar and went across town to a large concrete building — gray, anonymous, heavily barred, and set back from the street. This was the office and storage facility of Benny's Business Supplies, a company specializing in weapons and accessories, from assault rifles to magnetic self-detonating grenades. The proprietor, a jovial, round-faced German named Benny Schroeder, greeted them at the massive steel front door. "Good evening, boys," he said, while looking curiously at Sam. "Going hunting again, are you? Come in, come in."

He led them through to his office, which might have belonged to a senior bank executive — thick carpet, tasteful prints on the walls, and not a trace of anything deadly.

Schroeder beamed at them from across his desk. "Haven't seen you boys for a long time. What can I do for you?"

"Nothing too complicated," said Flo. "But we'll need it quickly — tomorrow or the next day at the latest."

"We'll go down to the cellar and you can see what we have in stock. But first, a little *schnapps*." He giggled. "I never do business on an empty stomach."

As they left Benny's with an old canvas bag holding their purchases, Sam suddenly stopped. "There's enough equipment in that place to start World War III. Isn't Benny ever bothered by the police?"

Flo smiled and shook his head. "They're his biggest customers."

The following morning, on the dot of ten, the Figatellis arrived at Nino Zonza's house for their first meeting with the Oblomovs. Coffee was served, and the four men inspected one another with cautious interest. Zonza began the meeting by advising them to carry out their reconnaissance of Speloncato before Reboul's arrival. He gave them a street plan of the village with the house of Madame Lombard, Reboul's aunt, circled in red. As part of the service, he also told them about the village's famous grottos, where all kinds of dark deeds had been committed over the centuries.

Zonza then listened carefully while they discussed their plans for the day: a trip to the village, of course, and a thorough reconnaissance of the roads around Spelon-cato to see if there were any likely spots for an ambush. Next, the question of identifying Reboul. No problem, said the Figatellis, we'll point him out when he arrives at the airport. Finally, there was the important matter of weapons. The Oblomovs had not wanted to risk trying to bring anything through airport security, and they were very particular about what they wanted — handguns, ideally with ten-round magazines, Glocks preferably. The Figatellis, with the memory of Benny Schroeder's cellar and its array of Glocks fresh in their minds, were able once again to say no problem. The four of them took their leave of Zonza, and set off. It was going to be a busy day.

Sam had almost lost count of the number of quick trips he had made to Calvi. He was now on his way back to Marseille for one last meeting with Reboul, to lay out his plans for the next few days. To his surprise and delight, he found Elena waiting for him at the airport.

"I was going to take a taxi," he said, kissing Elena, "but they don't have drivers like you."

"I'm good, but I'm expensive," she said. "A huge tip, plus dinner."

They got into the car for the half-hour drive to the city, but instead of moving off, Elena sat back in the driver's seat and folded her arms. "Right. We're not going anywhere until you tell me what you're up to."

Sam sighed. "OK. But I'll need your help, because this is going to be a tough sale." Elena started the engine and nosed her way into the airport traffic as Sam continued. "The more I look at this situation, the more I'm sure it's no place for the optimistic amateur. I don't think we should let Francis put himself on the line. Too many things could go wrong."

Elena nodded agreement, but said nothing.

"So what I want to do is take his place. I've worked everything out with Flo and Jo. We know exactly what we're going to do, and so all we have to do is persuade Francis. And you can help." He reached over and patted her thigh. "I'm told you're quite persuasive when you want to be."

Elena was frowning as she took in what Sam had said, conflicting thoughts filling her head. Of course she would like to see Francis kept well away from the Oblomovs. But at what risk to Sam?

"Are you sure about this?" she said. "Isn't there anything else we can do? Sam, I like you all in one piece."

The rest of the drive into Marseille was taken up by what amounted to a monologue from Sam. He went through the alternatives and he described, in detail, what he and the Figatellis planned to do, and how they were going to do it. And, just as they were pulling into Le Pharo, he admitted that he was thoroughly enjoying it all. "You know how it is," he said. "Guys just like to have fun."

Elena was still shaking her head as they went into the house.

Reboul's chef, Alphonse, had insisted that the host and his guests eat that evening at Le Pharo. One of his friends, a man whom Alphonse described as a very senior person in the fish world, *"un véritable maître de poissons,"* had given him some prime lobsters from Brittany, still alive and smelling of the sea. And of course, said Alphonse, they must be cooked and eaten fresh. Anything else would be a crime.

They were on the terrace having a glass of Sancerre when Sam decided it was time to start his pitch to Reboul.

"Francis, don't take this the wrong way, but I think I should take your place in Corsica." Sam paused to gauge Reboul's response, which was not immediately encouraging. "But before you tell me to get lost, let me tell you why. It's not about courage or character or that nonsense about a man's got to do what a man's got to do. It's about common sense and experience. Let's say you have a leaking bath. You don't try to fix it yourself; you call a plumber. With the situation we have here, Vronsky's the leaking bath and I'm the plumber. I've had years of experience doing this kind of thing, and you haven't. I have two first-class helpers in Flo and Jo, and I'm confident that the plan we have will work. So what I'm suggesting is that I go over to Corsica tomorrow on your plane, the Figatellis will point me out as you when I get off, and we'll take it from there." Sam stopped to drink some wine. "Also, I have to admit it — I actually enjoy these little adventures. So please say yes and wish me luck."

Reboul took a great deal more convincing. They were having coffee before he ran out of arguments, and turned to Elena. "What do you think?"

Elena shrugged. "I think Sam's right. You'll be doing us all a favor if you say yes."

Reboul stood up, moved along to Sam's chair, bent over and kissed the top of his head. "Thank you, Sam."

The Figatellis had spent seven hours with the Oblomovs and their day still wasn't over, since Zonza had requested a daily progress report.

"Well," he asked, "how are you getting on with your new colleagues?"

"Fine," said Jo. "They seem like a couple of pros, and they asked the right questions — in particular, how we were going to keep track of Reboul's comings and goings. Obviously, we need to know where he'll be before we can plan anything."

"Of course," said Zonza. "So what did you tell them?"

Jo's face, as always when he was telling a lie, was a study in honest innocence. "I suddenly remembered that I have a young niece who works for Madame Lombard as a housemaid."

"How convenient," said Zonza.

"Isn't it? So she can tell us exactly when he leaves the house and where he's going," said Jo.

"Excellent."

"Tomorrow we're testing the equipment, and I'm sure that by the end of the day our little house-maid will have some news."

Zonza bared his gold teeth in what passed for a smile. "So far, so good. Keep it up."

When the Figatellis had gone, Zonza allowed himself a few moments of satisfaction. He was now quite comfortable about having changed sides. He had never taken to the Oblomovs; too crude, too brutish. The Figatellis, on the other hand, could be relied on to remember his cooperation with gratitude. And in Corsica, favors, like grudges, were valid for many years. Finally, the financial side was not without its attractions. The Oblomovs had already paid 50 percent of a substantial fee, which they would forfeit, and the Figatellis had assured Zonza that there would be more to come from Reboul. It was a most satisfactory state of affairs.

CHAPTER EIGHTEEN

"Well," said Sam, "this is the Corsican outfit." He stood in front of Elena, hands in his pockets, a wide-brim Panama hat on his head, and very large, very dark sunglasses on his nose. He was wearing a pale-blue shirt and white pants, the uniform of the relaxed gentleman in the South of France. "The idea of all this," he said, "is to make myself recognizable to the Oblomovs from a distance, but at the same time hiding a lot of my face.

What do you think?"

Elena gave him a suitably thorough inspection, and nodded. "You'll do," she said. "But promise me you'll be careful. No heroics, OK? Now take off those goddam sunglasses so I can give you a good-luck kiss." And a long, serious kiss it was.

"That was interesting," said Sam. "What do I get if I take off my hat?"

They went downstairs to join Reboul, who had insisted on coming with them. He would act, as he said, as Elena's bodyguard while Sam was otherwise occupied. The two of them would be staying at the Villa Prestige, a high-security, high-luxury house a few minutes' drive from the center of Calvi.

They settled three abreast in the back of the car that was taking them to the area reserved for private planes at the Marseille airport. During the drive, Sam took them through, once again, what would happen when they landed in Calvi. Elena and Reboul were to wait in the plane until Sam had left the airport. Once off the plane, Sam would get into the waiting car that had been organized by the Figatellis — a large Peugeot, distinctive because of its densely tinted windows. This would take him to Madame Lombard's house in Speloncato while Reboul and Elena were taken to the Villa Prestige.

The short flight to Corsica was subdued and, now that the action had begun, increasingly tense. Reboul was restless, fidgeting with his cell phone. Elena was silent, clutching Sam's hand and staring out the window. Sam had disappeared into a bubble of concentration, as he always did before a job. He went over the meticulous arrangements he had made with the Figatellis. In theory, he reckoned, they had covered every possibility. And yet, you can never be sure. Wherever you have goons and guns, mistakes can happen. But still — it's the element of risk that makes the whole thing worth doing. And on that philosophical note he left his bubble, leaned over, and kissed Elena's ear.

The plane set down with barely a bump. By the time the door was opened, the Peugeot was already coming across the tarmac toward them. Sam left the plane, taking his time as he went down the steps to give anyone watching from the terminal a good look at him, and greeted the chauffeur standing by the open rear door. This was one of the older members of the Figatelli clan, Uncle Doumé, a squat, leathery man with a sweet, crooked smile and an impressive pair of shaggy white eyebrows. He took Sam's bag, and they set off on the winding road to Speloncato.

Back in the terminal, Sasha Oblomov lowered his binoculars with a grunt. "I was expecting someone older," he said to the Figatellis. "He looks younger than he did in the photographs."

"Ah," said Flo, "they were probably taken before the face-lift — you know what these rich guys are like. I guess he'll be going straight to Speloncato. No need to follow him, unless you want to?"

Oblomov shook his head. "We have plenty of time," he said. "I want to go somewhere we can try out the guns."

They drove out of the airport and into the deserted countryside of the Balagna, parking in the shade of a scrub oak before pushing their way through tangles of *maquis* and into a small clearing. Jo unpacked the guns and handed one of them to Sasha. The other he held up as he went into his explanation.

"I think you'll like this: the Glock 23," he said. "Light, reliable, used by the police all over America. The magazine holds thirteen rounds, the safety is here" — he clicked the safety catch off and on — "and that's about all you need to know. Let me load them and set up a target and you can try them out. Oh, I almost forgot. These guns just got into Corsica last night, and they're new. This evening I need to take them to a guy we've often used and have him file off the serial numbers. Just a precaution we like to take."

The Oblomovs nodded their approval of this evidence of professional discretion.

The guns were loaded and the

targets — beer cans from six-packs bought by the Figatellis — set up. The Oblomovs started firing, slowly at first and then, as they got used to the guns, more rapidly. It was immediately clear that both of them were comfortable with weapons, and that they were good marksmen. As the bullets flew and the beer cans jumped, Flo's earlier impression was confirmed. These two were no amateurs.

The Oblomovs had begun to show some enthusiasm, nodding and smiling and clapping each other on the back. Half a dozen magazines later, they were satisfied, and handed the guns back. The atmosphere between the Oblomovs and the Figatellis, if not exactly warm, had become cordial. They all agreed that useful progress had been made: the victim identified, the weapons tested and found excellent. Now they needed to find the perfect spot, and a prime opportunity. The Figatellis said they would consult with their niece about the victim's movements to help them pick a time.

Sam, never comfortable with violent changes of direction, whether by boat, plane, or car, did his best to keep smiling as Uncle Doumé hurled the Peugeot around ever tighter bends, the car horn at full blast. Speloncato, which he hoped to reach alive, sits at two thousand feet above sea level, with a permanent population, according to the latest count, of 280. It has one principal claim to fame: its grottos. Moist and gloomy, they had been the scene of many dark deeds, so the guidebook said. A frustration for the curious reader, thirsty for knowledge, was that no details of the dark deeds were provided. Sam consoled himself with the thought that Reboul's aunt, Madame Lombard, would be sure to tell him.

After what Reboul had told him about his aunt, Sam was very much looking forward to meeting her. The daughter of a diplomat who had been posted to England, she had been educated at Roedean, one of the top girls' schools in the country, where she had learned to play field hockey, which she detested, and to speak perfect English with the languid drawl of the upper classes. She was now in her seventies. She had never married but, according to Reboul, had had her fair share of lovers. She spent her summers in the old family house in Speloncato, her winters in Gstaad, and the rest of the year in Paris.

Arriving at the small *place* in the center of the village, Uncle Doumé pulled up in front of a four-story mansion the color of dark ochre, and announced his arrival with a final triumphant bellow from his horn. Almost at once, the front door opened and a sturdy young woman peered out, her face lighting up as she recognized Uncle

Doumé.

He opened his arms as he walked toward her. "Josette! Beautiful as ever!" He kissed her cheeks three times — left, right, left — and stepped back to introduce Sam. "This is Monsieur Sam, a friend of Monsieur Francis in Marseille. Madame Lombard is expecting him."

Josette ducked her head, shook hands with Sam, and took his bag. "Madame is in the *salon*. Please. This way." She led them through a tiled entrance hall and into a vast room at the back of the house, furnished in the heavy, ornate style of a long-ago era — velvet, mahogany, brocade, swagged curtains, gilt-framed family portraits. Sam felt as if he had stepped back into the nineteenth century.

Madame Lombard looked up from her writing desk and came toward Sam, smiling and extending one elegant hand, which he bent over to kiss.

"Good heavens," she said. "Do you still kiss hands in America? How nice. Here — come and sit down."

It was hard to believe that this was a woman in her seventies. She had gray hair, certainly, short and beautifully cut. But the skin on her face was smooth, the blue eyes lively, the body as slender as a young woman's. She was dressed simply, in a black silk shirt and a cream-colored skirt that set off the tan on her excellent legs. Sam realized he'd been staring.

"Well," she said, "what were you expecting? Some old crone with a pince-nez and a moustache?"

"Excuse me, I'm sorry. I just wasn't expecting . . . well, someone who looks like you."

She smiled. "I'll take that as a compliment. Now, Francis has told me very little except that you're American, and you're doing him an enormous favor. Naturally, I'm agog to know more." She waved her hand toward the ice bucket on the low table between them. "Why don't you pour us a glass of Champagne and tell me all about it?"

They talked well into the evening. At first, when Sam described Vronsky and what he intended to do, Madame Lombard sat quietly, her face set and serious. "But surely," she said, "he's not prepared to arrange a murder just to get a house?"

"I'm afraid so," said Sam, "if his past history is anything to go by. But we're not going to let that happen." And, over the next half hour, he explained to her exactly what he and the Figatellis were going to do.

After he'd finished, she was greatly relieved, even more so after another glass of Champagne. As they continued to talk, she instructed Sam to call her Laura, while she had begun to call him "dear boy." She was asking him what she could do to help when they were interrupted by the sound of loud scratching at the door.

"Ah," said Laura, as she went to open the door, "I do hope you like dogs. This is Alfred, the man in my life. Isn't he splendid?"

He was huge and black and shaggy, a cross, so Laura said, between a briard and a Rottweiler. He padded across to Sam, inspected him, sniffed him, put one massive paw on his knee, and looked up at him expectantly.

"He likes you," said Laura. "I *am* glad. He's such a good judge of character. I had a gentleman friend once whom Alfred absolutely loathed. And do you know, he was quite right. The man turned out to be a dreadful little shit."

Sam was wondering how to disengage his knee from the paw without causing offense when the cook put her head around the door to announce dinner.

Over some well-turned lamb chops, salad, cheese, and a bottle of Château Margaux — "I find the local wines rather *fierce,*" said Laura — the conversation became serious again, and she repeated her wish to help.

"There are a couple of things," said Sam. "First, I need to find a place where I can be ambushed; somewhere deserted, obviously. And second, I need to have a reason for wandering around in the middle of nowhere. Otherwise, I'm worried that the Oblomovs will smell a rat."

"Nothing could be easier," said Laura. "I can show you exactly where to go, and your reason for going is sitting on your foot. That shows he really *does* like you. Why don't you take him for a walk tomorrow?"

Over coffee, the details were worked out. Sam would call Jo and tell him where and when he would be walking the dog. Jo would tell the Oblomovs that his niece had given him the information, and they would arrange to hide themselves close to where Sam would be walking. After that, as Sam said, it would be all over bar the shooting.

CHAPTER NINETEEN

After his first-ever night in a four-poster bed, Sam was woken up by the sun streaming through an open window. He felt alert and pleasantly tense, as he always did when close to the climax of an operation. A warm and soothing soak in a venerable cast-iron bathtub helped him relax, and then he started on the day's phone calls.

"Good morning, sweetheart. How do you like roughing it in Calvi?"

"Sam, it's wonderful. Private

pool, great cooking, and wait till you see my dressing room. It's *enormous.* I love it. I almost got lost in it."

Sam had never before heard Elena wax lyrical about a place to hang her clothes. Usually, she complained about lack of space; this was a rare sign of approval. "Tell me, how is Francis?"

"He's OK. A bit edgy, but I guess that's to be expected. And he's very worried about you. What are you doing today?"

"Oh, exploring the countryside, finding a place to be ambushed, setting everything up with Flo and Jo, dealing with the Russians — just a normal day in the life of a busy executive."

Elena could sense from Sam's voice that his mind was very much elsewhere, so after telling him once again to be extra careful, she ended the call with a kiss blown down the line.

Sam went downstairs in search of coffee, and was surprised to find his hostess already sitting at the dining table, croissant and *café crème* by her side, a laptop in front of her. This was her way of catching up on the news of the day, she explained, since the nearest available newspaper was miles away in Calvi.

"You're going to be very pleased with me, dear boy," she said. "I think I know exactly where you should go to be ambushed." She started to tap the laptop's keyboard. "Now, get yourself a cup of coffee from that pot on the sideboard and come and sit next to me."

She moved the laptop so that Sam had a better view of the screen, which showed an aerial view of dense green treetops and vegetation. "This is typical of the countryside around Speloncato," she said. "Most of it is no good for you because there are no paths, and finding a particular spot would be impossible for anyone who didn't know the area. But this" — she scrolled down the screen — "this is much better. It's a reservoir about nine kilometers down the road, not difficult to find, and surrounded by *maquis* and abandoned olive groves, so there would be plenty of places for those ghastly Russians to lurk."

Sam leaned forward to take a closer look at the image on the screen. "Isn't that a path, quite wide, there on the left?"

Laura nodded. "It leads down from the road, but the only people who use it, once every six months or so, are the maintenance men for the reservoir." She sat back, a smile of satisfaction on her face. "Well, do you think that will do?"

"I'll go and check it out this morning, but it looks terrific. How can I thank you? Let's see now, would a magnum of Dom Pérignon be acceptable?"

Laura, still smiling, inclined her head. "How delightful. Magnums are so comforting, don't you think?"

Half an hour later, Sam set off in an elderly Renault borrowed from the gardener. Following the road that wound down from the village, he came to the entrance to the path, marked by a rusting sign that read *Accès Interdit.* He parked the car on the grass and began walking.

Almost everywhere he looked there were tiny clearings between the overgrown, neglected olive trees, ideal spots in which to hide and wait. The reservoir itself, a grim oasis of insect-speckled water, was surrounded by mesh fencing, with a squat concrete blockhouse at one end, locked and, Sam thought, of no great interest to the ambushers. There were dozens of other, more suitable places. And the location couldn't be better, easy to find and yet secluded, with no chance of shots being heard. Perfect. Sam found an old tree stump to sit on, and called Jo Figatelli.

There were a few details to finalize, and these were agreed upon over the course of the next few minutes. Jo and Flo would drive over from Calvi later that morning to familiarize themselves with the area around the reservoir, and they would call the Oblomovs to suggest a time for the ambush. Jo confirmed that they would bring what he described as "all the necessary equipment," told Sam to remember to dust off his bulletproof vest, and said he'd call again in the afternoon, once he'd spoken to the Oblomovs.

The phone was answered with a grunt. Which Oblomov was it? Jo took a chance. "Sasha, it's Jo Figatelli, with some good news. I've just had a call from my niece in Speloncato. She heard Reboul talking to Madame Lombard, saying he'd like to take her dog out for a walk this evening. He asked her where to go, and she recommended the local reservoir, about a five-minute drive down from the village. It sounds good. We're on our way to take a look at it now. I'll call you back. Meanwhile, how does the timing sound to you? Is this evening OK?"

"Yes," said Oblomov. "Have you got the merchandise back?"

"Later on this morning."

"Good," said the Russian, and the line went dead.

Jo looked over at his brother, who was driving. "Next time, you call him. Maybe he won't be so long-winded with you."

They parked at the entrance to the path, and walked down toward the reservoir. "This is fine," said Flo, "but we need to find somewhere to hide our car. Sam's not going to walk all the way from the village with the dog. He'll drive and park at the top of the path, and if our car is already there, the Oblomovs will think we're giving the game away. There must be a place down here where the maintenance guys park when they come to the reservoir."

In fact, they were walking straight toward it — a space behind the blockhouse with a rudimentary parking area covered in cracked concrete that was fighting a losing battle against the weeds.

"OK," said Jo, "that'll do. Now we need somewhere we can hide the Russians where Sam can find them."

They quickly saw that they were spoiled for choice. There were clearings between clumps of trees, there was waist-high *maquis,* there were even a few narrow tracks that had been made by hunters. The Figatellis explored one of these tracks leading off from the parking area and found that, after about three hundred yards, it came to a small clearing surrounded by plenty of cover. Couldn't be better, they both agreed. On their way back, Jo came across a crumpled, discarded cigarette pack, which he placed at the entrance to the chosen track as a marker to help Sam set off in the right direction.

All that remained to be done was to pick up the guns and call Sam to tell him about the cigarette pack. They might even have time for lunch before installing the Oblomovs in their hiding place.

■ ■ ■ ■

The afternoon was passing slowly
for Sam. He had long conversations
with Elena, Reboul, and Jo Figatelli, and was then pleased to be
distracted by Laura, who insisted
on giving him dog-walking lessons.
These were endured rather than
enjoyed by Alfred, who had been
through them all before.

"My advice," said Laura, "is to
keep him on the leash until you get
a good way down the path. You
don't want him rushing off after a
rabbit. It might help if you had a
few of these. He's addicted to
them." She gave Sam half a dozen
bone-shaped dog biscuits, which he
put in his pocket. The watchful

Alfred immediately came over to him and started to nudge the bulging pocket with his nose. "Now that he knows you've got them he won't let you out of his sight. Such a greedy boy."

Finally, it was time. Sam put on the bulletproof vest, then his shirt, his hat, and his sunglasses. Laura walked him out to the car, saw Alfred installed on the passenger seat, and leaned through the window to kiss Sam's cheek. "Good luck, dear boy. I'll have the Champagne on ice when you get back."

Flo Figatelli, from a vantage point in the bushes by the side of the road, saw Sam's car coming toward the reservoir. He called his brother as he hurried back to join him and the Oblomovs.

"He's just about at the top of the path," said Jo. "Another five minutes and he'll be down here." The Oblomovs nodded and took out their guns. This was turning out to be easier than they had expected. They squatted behind their bush, making sure their field of fire wouldn't be blocked by any thick foliage.

Halfway down the path, Sam let Alfred off the leash. The dog rummaged in the bushes, delighted to find unfamiliar smells, coming back every few minutes to make sure that Sam and his precious supply of biscuits weren't too far away. They reached the reservoir, found the cigarette pack, and started off down the track, Alfred leading the way.

Sam's mind was clear, his senses on full alert, his eyes fixed on Alfred's shaggy rump. The dog would be the first, Sam reckoned, to sense any sign of the presence of human life in the undergrowth. Something crunched under his foot, and he looked down to see a small heap of hunters' droppings — empty shotgun cartridge cases that had been partly stamped into the earth. After another few yards, there was an empty *pastis* flask. Thirsty work, hunting. On they went, following the twists of the track until they could see, fifty yards ahead, the opening of the clearing.

Alfred stopped. His head lowered, he resumed walking toward the clearing with deliberate, stiff-legged steps, as though he had already seen something, and was stalking it. Sam braced himself as they came to the end of the path. Alfred stopped again, his attention focused on a clump of bushes a few feet ahead.

The Oblomovs, hidden in that very clump, were of two minds. Should they shoot the dog first, or the man? Sign language from the elder Oblomov indicated the man. They were being paid to shoot the man; the dog they would dispose of later. They raised their guns and took aim.

The two shots came within a split

second of each other. Sam's body jackknifed as he fell to the ground, facedown, with Alfred whining beside him. The bushes parted, and out came the Oblomovs, guns at the ready, unaware of the Figatellis closing up behind them, each carrying a "Corsican persuader" — a short, blunt wooden club with a solid-lead head. The Oblomovs, intent on Sam's motionless body, never saw the blows coming. They dropped instantly.

"Nice work, guys." Sam sat up, rubbing his chest and trying to ward off Alfred, who was licking his face. "Ouf! I never thought those blanks would carry such a wallop. Lucky I was wearing the vest. OK, let's get them ready for their big moment."

The Oblomovs showed no signs of consciousness as they were rolled over and their hands were cuffed behind their backs. Their cell phones were taken, and their guns were transferred to plastic bags, using handkerchiefs to avoid leaving prints. Flo took out his phone. "You can come down now," he said. "They'll wake up in a couple of minutes."

They were bleary-eyed but conscious by the time the big Peugeot with the darkened windows arrived and pulled to a stop. The driver, a large man with a boxer's broken nose, got out and opened the rear door, and Uncle Doumé emerged. Sam hardly recognized him. Gone were the old work clothes, the sweet smile, and three days' worth of stubble. This, judging by his dark suit and even darker sunglasses, was a man of some importance. He walked slowly over to the Oblomovs and stood looking down at them, his hands on his hips. "So," he said, "these are the killers." He turned his head. "Claude — my chair."

The driver came over from the car carrying a director's chair, unfolded it and placed it in front of the Oblomovs. Uncle Doumé sat down and took a small cheroot from his pocket, lit it carefully, and blew on the end until it glowed.

"You have placed yourselves in a difficult and dangerous situation," he said to the Oblomovs. "You have attempted to murder my good friend here" — he waved his cheroot in Sam's direction — "an attempt which he and his colleagues have prevented. They are now witnesses who will be happy to testify against you. As further proof, your fingerprints are all over the weapons. And you are in Corsica, where this kind of behavior is not tolerated, particularly not from foreigners."

He paused, and blew a smoke ring. "As I said, a dangerous situation. It seems to me that there are a number of options, some less pleasant than others. First, we could shoot you, and claim self-defense." The Oblomovs were beginning to show signs of apprehension. "Second, we could have you tried for attempted murder in front of a friend of mine, a judge, and I can promise that he would hand down a harsh sentence — thirty or forty years in a Corsican jail. And third, the most sensible option: you cooperate with us, and your reward would be a very much lighter sentence, to be served, if you prefer, in France. Do you have any questions?"

There was no response from the Oblomovs.

"Good. I will leave you with my colleagues, but I warn you. They are not patient men." And with that, Uncle Doumé returned to his car. Claude folded up the chair and followed.

Not surprisingly, after a very brief discussion the Oblomovs chose the third option. Jo Figatelli called one of his many close contacts at police headquarters in Calvi and arranged for a van to be sent to pick up the Russians and take them to be locked up pending interrogation.

"We'll wait for them here," said Jo to Sam. "You've done your work for the day. Go back to the house and have a drink."

Sam sat in the car, gave Alfred a celebratory biscuit, and called Elena. "It's done, and everything went according to plan. The Russians are on their way to jail."

Elena's sigh was a huge gust of relief. "Are you OK?"

317

"I have a mild case of bulletproof-vest rash, but otherwise I'm fine. I'm on my way back to Laura's house. I'll tell you all about it over dinner."

There was another long sigh. "Sam, I've been so worried."

"I'll be fine. The rash usually clears up after a couple of days."

The first thing that Sam saw when he got back was the big Peugeot parked in front of the house. A close second was the welcoming committee of Uncle Doumé, Laura, Elena, and Reboul waiting by the open front door. Alfred bounded from the car, with Sam following. He hugged Elena, and felt warm tears on her cheeks. Reboul embraced him, patted his back, squeezed his shoulder, ruffled his hair, and looked as though he might burst into tears himself. A perfumed kiss from Laura, a smile and a grunt from Uncle Doumé, and they went into the house.

Reboul was almost dancing with relief and excitement, and Elena was gripping Sam's hand so tightly he thought he should ask her to stop before it came off. Laura and Uncle Doumé, nodding and smiling, added to the general air of merriment as they went into the living room and gathered around a magnum of Champagne in its oversized ice bucket. While Reboul was dealing with the cork, Sam felt it was time for a quick dose of reality.

"I hate to say this," he said, "but

let's not overdo the celebration just yet. It's not over. We still have to deal with Vronsky."

CHAPTER TWENTY

Before Sam could get any further into the problem of Vronsky, his phone rang.

"Jo? What happened?" Sam wedged the phone more firmly against his ear. "They did? Both of them? That's great. Don't let them anywhere near a phone. I think we can get going now. I'll talk to you later."

He was smiling as he put down the phone. "Good news. In return for reduced sentences, the Oblomovs have both signed confessions that they were carrying out an assassination contract for Vronsky. That makes him an accomplice in an attempted murder, and that just about does it. I think I could manage a drink."

Reboul poured, Sam drank. Champagne had never tasted so good.

"I have a little news of my own," said Reboul. "You know my friend Hervé? He's explained everything to his counterpart in Paris, and the Paris flics are ready to move on Vronsky as soon as you give the word."

"The sooner the better," said Sam. "There's nothing to be gained by waiting, and Vronsky will start getting nervous when he doesn't hear from the Oblomovs. Does Hervé work late? Could we call him now?"

Five minutes later, it was all arranged. The police would pick Vronsky up as he left the Bristol to go out to dinner. He would spend the night in a Parisian cell. The following day, he would be delivered to Marseille, where he would face interrogation and trial. Hervé said that with a word in the right ear, it could be arranged for Vronsky to be sent to French Guiana, on the coast of South America, to serve his sentence. A most unhealthy place, according to Hervé, where the odds against survival were high.

"Now, my friends," Reboul said,

"do you think it's safe to celebrate? Because I have a suggestion: lunch at Le Pharo, perhaps the day after tomorrow, so that my chef has time to prepare. I will arrange transport for everyone from Calvi to Marseille. How does that sound? Only if you're free, of course." He looked around at the smiling faces of Laura, Doumé, Elena, and Sam. "And we mustn't forget the Figatelli boys."

The following morning, the three of them boarded Reboul's plane for the short hop back to Marseille. Reboul was still effervescent with relief, even more so when Hervé called to say that Vronsky had been picked up as planned and would be delivered to Marseille later in the day. He had apparently been threatening massive lawsuits for wrongful arrest to anyone who cared to listen.

"He can squawk all he wants to," said Reboul, "but he doesn't know yet about those signed confessions. Sam, I didn't want to ask you before — but were you absolutely sure those guns had been loaded with blanks?"

"Of course," said Sam. "The Figatellis knew that if they screwed up I'd come back to haunt them. Seriously, they were terrific. They loaded the magazines themselves, and found some way of keeping the guns out of the Oblomovs' hands until the last minute. I never had any worries."

Half an hour later, they were in the car, heading back to Le Pharo. Reboul immediately went into the kitchen for a conference with Alphonse, planning the menu for the celebration lunch. Elena and Sam went down to the pool and stretched out in the sun.

"I still can't believe it's all over," said Elena. She leaned over and kissed Sam on the tip of his nose. "Can we go back to having a vacation now?"

"What do you have in mind?"

"Just the usual stuff. You know, making love in the afternoon, dinner under the stars, that kind of thing. Maybe we could look at a few apartments, explore the *calanques,* spend some time with Mimi and Philippe."

"Anything you want, my sweet, as long as I don't have to wear a bulletproof vest. What happened to that, by the way?"

"Laura took it and put it in Alfred's basket. She said the scent of it would remind him of you."

Sam was considering this unusual compliment when Reboul arrived at the pool, smiling broadly and clutching a sheet of paper. *"Voilà,"* he said, waving the paper, "Alphonse and I have agreed on the menu for tomorrow, and it is a *tour de force.* I won't spoil his moment by telling you the details — he wants to do that himself — but I can guarantee a most memorable meal, a banquet. And now, I must go to the cellar and choose the wines." He paused, and gave a long, theatrical sigh. "My work is never done."

The group making its way up the steps of Reboul's plane the following morning provided an interesting contrast in dress styles. Laura, elegant in gray silk; Uncle Doumé in a flowered shirt and baggy white trousers; the Figatellis in jeans and their favorite T-shirts, black with gold lettering spelling out the reassuring promise that whatever happens in Vegas stays in Vegas.

The short trip over to Marseille gave Laura, who had never met the Figatellis, the chance to get to know them. She clearly liked what she saw, and flirted outrageously. They flirted back, and she became quite girlish, with much fluttering of the eyelashes. Uncle Doumé was busy in the cockpit taking beginner's lessons from the pilot, and by the time the plane landed everyone was in the best of spirits.

Le Pharo was ready for them. Reboul, with decorating advice offered by Elena, had turned one corner of the terrace into a haven of shade, with giant umbrellas shielding a seating area and the long dining table from the sun. White was everywhere — the umbrellas, the armchairs and couches, the tablecloth and napkins, and the 'Iceberg' roses that overflowed from huge terra-cotta pots. Elena and Reboul had dressed to match, all in white.

"Bravo, Francis, bravo." Laura patted Reboul on the cheek. "This is quite wonderful, just like something out of that magazine — what's it called? — *Côté Sud.* Now then, if someone were to offer me a little of that excellent Champagne I see on the table, I don't think I could resist."

Reboul had arranged for Claudine, his housekeeper, and Nanou, his housemaid from Martinique, to take care of his guests, and when he saw that everyone had a glass he stood up to offer a few words of welcome.

"First, let me say how grateful I

am to you all for your help. Nobody could ask for better friends, and I shall never forget what you've done. This lunch, this happy occasion, is to say thank you, but I also want to say that if ever there is anything I can do to help any of you, all you have to do is ask." He paused, a little emotional, and swallowed hard before continuing. "It is a day to eat, drink, and be merry. Never has a fine meal been so richly de-served. And now, to prepare you for what is to come, it's time to wel-come Alphonse, king of Le Pharo's kitchen and creator of today's menu."

The chef, who had been waiting outside the kitchen door for his cue, came forward, smiling and nodding at the guests.

Alphonse, as Elena later re-marked, restored one's faith in the classic French chef — classically rotund, classically jolly, and wear-ing a long, heavy apron instead of the dainty white monogrammed jackets so popular with show busi-ness chefs. He made his way onto the terrace accompanied by a round of applause, took his place next to Reboul, and cleared his throat.

"I have prepared for you a simple lunch with, as you will see, one or two Corsican touches in honor of our Corsican friends." He nodded and beamed at the Figatellis and Uncle Doumé. "To start, *coquilles Saint-Jacques* to awaken the palate

— just three per person, pan-fried, and accompanied by chives and a *ragoût* of new peas and broad beans, drizzled with olive oil and the merest dusting of Camargue salt."

He took a sip of the Champagne that Reboul had passed to him before moving on to the next course. "We remain with the saints, and with the appetite now on the *qui vive,* we have a *filet de Saint-Pierre,* with asparagus tips and a lemon emulsion, made, *naturelle-ment,* with the finest Corsican lemons." Another nod and a beam to the Figatellis.

"To follow, braised rump of Corsican veal, with a *fricassée* of new potatoes and carrots and an infused *jus* of savory. This will put us in the mood for a selection of goat cheeses, and here, I must confess, I cannot promise that all the goats who contributed were Corsican. Even so, I think you will enjoy the cheeses. There are three: one soft and creamy; one hard and strong; and one *cendré,* with a fine dusting of ashes. The combination is subtle and delicious."

He looked toward Laura, and bowed his head. "To finish, I am indebted to Madame Lombard, who gave me the recipe for her sublime chocolate cake, rich and dark. I have added some early-season cherries, stoned and lightly heated in Corsican *myrte* until the juices run, and a large flourish of whipped cream." He looked around, smiling at his audience, and delivered the traditional chef's blessing, *"Alors, bon appétit!"* The applause followed him back to the kitchen.

Elena was shaking her head at Sam. "If that's a simple lunch, I'm Paul Bocuse. You're going to have to carry me away from the table."

Reboul, who had been standing next to them, pretended to be shocked. "No, no, no," he said. "I know the list of dishes is long, but the portions are modest, a series of exquisite mouthfuls. After you've eaten, you will spring from the table, ready for a run around the Vieux Port." He cocked his head and winked. "Or possibly a siesta."

"Now you're talking," said Elena.

A good lunch anywhere is a pleasure, but a good lunch with friends out of doors on a fine summer's day is a total joy. Everything seems to have been given an extra touch of magic. The wine tastes better, the jokes are funnier, the compliments more elegant, the food more delicious. And so it was that day at Le Pharo. The gastronomic voyage from *coquilles Saint-Jacques* to Laura's chocolate triumph took three hours, with interludes between courses for impromptu speeches, most of which were in fact extended invitations. Sam and Elena invited everyone to Los Angeles. The Figatellis invited everyone to Calvi. Laura offered a choice

336

between Paris and Gstaad, and Uncle Doumé proposed a visit to his family's vineyard in Patrimonio, where, he said, even the bathroom taps ran with wine.

Reboul had just gotten to his feet when his phone rang. He stood at the head of the table, listening intently, smiling at first and then laughing out loud. He was shaking his head as the call finished. "I can promise you a rare sight, my friends," he said. "Follow me." He led the group to the edge of the terrace, scooping up a pair of binoculars from a low table, and stood looking out to sea. "The call was from Hervé," he said. "Any moment now, we should see them coming round the headland."

A minute passed, then two, and finally they saw, rounding the headland a few hundred yards away, a dark-blue police launch. It was dwarfed by what was following it — *The Caspian Queen,* her Russian ensign at half-mast. The binoculars were passed around, and it was possible to make out several figures dressed in the uniform of the Police Nationale moving around the main deck.

"They're on their way to the port," said Reboul, "where Hervé tells me the boat will be kept while — how did he put it? — the owner is helping the police with their inquiries. So I don't think we'll be seeing any more of *The Caspian Queen.*"

"I'll drink to that," said Sam. "Champagne, anyone?"

ABOUT THE AUTHOR

Peter Mayle is the author of thirteen previous books, seven of them novels. A recipient of the Légion d'Honneur from the French government for his cultural contributions, he has been living in Provence with his wife, Jennie, for twenty years.

The employees of Thorndike Press hope
you have enjoyed this Large Print book.
All our Thorndike, Wheeler, and Ken-
nebec Large Print titles are designed for
easy reading, and all our books are made
to last. Other Thorndike Press Large Print
books are available at your library, through
selected bookstores, or directly from us.

For information about titles, please call:
  (800) 223-1244

or visit our Web site at:
  http://gale.cengage.com/thorndike

To share your comments, please write:
  Publisher
  Thorndike Press
  10 Water St., Suite 310
  Waterville, ME 04901